TRIPLE AXE

SCOTT COLE

Other books by Scott Cole

SuperGhost

Slices: Tales of Bizarro and Absurdist Horror

Did I write this book? No. Am I still going to sign this book I didn't write? Yes. Is someone in this book Killed with a dildo? Also yes. 5 stars. Happy Birthday Kim!!

Justin

For all the dirty birds.

1

"Okay, honey, now scoot your ass over this way a bit. Arch your back more. Turn this way a little bit. Good. Put your left knee up here. Push your tits out. Yup. Now slide your other leg this way. Arms over your head . . . and . . . perfect. Now go to town, Brock."

Johnson Grande had a way with words. Jesse struggled to accommodate the director's instructions, but it wasn't exactly easy while hanging practically upside-down over a wooden chair with the back of it digging into her ribs. Unpleasant wasn't quite the word for it. But that's how it was with these shoots sometimes. Holding uncomfortable positions for extended periods of time, all while some sweaty muscle-bro pounded away at her from some equally strange angle. It all looked good on camera, though, and that's what it was about. The finished product. The end result.

Either of those could be titles, she thought. Jesse Jinx is . . . *The Finished Product*. Jesse Jinx in . . . *The End Result*. They'd have to be a bit more on the artsy side, though. A little classier than the shoot she was currently on.

Some day, she thought. Some day soon. Maybe six more months and she'd have enough money saved up to start her own production company. No more saying yes to every offer from every slimy director in the business. No more shady agents looking to skim from her paychecks. No more following the whims of every con man with a camera in his hand.

Not that she didn't enjoy her work. Jesse got into the business out of a love for sex and a penchant for being watched, whether it was live or recorded. And it beat the hell out of being an accountant. But the business side of things seemed to be spoiling the fun more often than not these days.

She wasn't looking to get out of porn. She was just looking for some more say, a bit more control over how it all worked. She planned to hire her friends and do things the way she wanted. Jinx Pix.

The pain in her side brought her back to the present moment. She punctuated her moans with a squeal of discomfort, but it only seemed to excite her dance partner more, and he began pumping faster. Jesse's candy apple-red hair now shook frantically from her scalp instead of cascading gently with the rhythm of Brock Longfinger's thrusts.

"Ooh, ooh . . . *Oww!*" she screamed. "*Owwwww!* Stop, stop. I need to get up." The beast inside her pulled out, and Jesse twisted and rolled off the edge of the chair, revealing a sharp pinkish-purple line across her side that would surely be darker by the next morning.

"What the fuck are you doing, Red?" the director screamed. "We're not done here."

"I gotta change positions, John," Jesse said, sweeping her long, unnaturally colored hair out of her face and over one shoulder. "Unless you want me to end up in the hospital."

"I don't care where you end up tonight, as long as I get this scene in the can. Get the fuck back up there," Johnson said sharply. He wasn't interested in anything other than finishing the day's work, no matter how much pain it caused. "Brock, I hope you're about ready to pop."

Brock grunted in the affirmative, sweat trickling down his temples, echoing the lines of his bulging forehead veins.

"Well at least give me a pillow or something," Jesse said, stretching her body in the opposite direction to the way she had been positioned on the chair. "I mean, you want me back tomorrow, right? At the very least, this is going to be a bruise."

"That's what the make-up girl is for, darling. She'll cover up your bruises the same way she covered up some of those nasty amateur tattoos. Airbrushing is a magical thing."

"Thanks so much for your concern," Jesse said, paying little mind to the insult. She loved her tattoos—the classic pinup girl on the inside of her forearm, the filigree design on her shoulder, and especially the bouquet of flowers adorning her entire left side. And they definitely weren't amateur.

She looked forward to a day when Johnson no longer had her number.

"Now can I please get a pillow? The pop shot's a close-up, right? It won't even be in frame."

"Peter! Fetch a pillow for the Red Queen, won't you? A *small* one!"

Jesse glanced across the room and saw her friend Selina standing in the doorway wearing only a thin robe, her arms crossed beneath her breasts. They rolled eyes at each other and knew they'd be discussing the afternoon's work over drinks later. Several drinks.

"Here you go, Miss Jinx," said Peter, the Production Assistant, as he proffered a small pillow with a beautifully embroidered flower pattern on it.

"Thanks, honey," Jesse said. She gave him a wink, then reassumed her position on the chair as best she could. She had to trust Brock to not let her fall, which normally wouldn't be a problem. But she also knew when he came, his mind might become a bit scrambled. So she held her position and braced for potential impact. It wouldn't be the first time.

A minute or so later, Brock grunted significantly louder than before and spat a steady stream of semen across Jesse's chest and face. He managed to keep a foot on the seat of the chair, though, which helped Jesse not to tumble to the floor in the process.

A drop of Brock's fluid hit Jesse's eye, and she screamed internally as the burning sensation set in. She wouldn't let the pain show, though. She was a professional. Besides, she didn't want to have to do this again a half hour later, let alone have to listen to whatever Johnson had to say about it.

"Damn," said Johnson, extending the word an extra couple seconds in disbelief, admiring the dozen or so heaves Brock had unloaded. "Okay then. That's lunch!"

"Can you believe this shit they feed us?" said Selina, staring at the sandwich in her hand from various angles like it was a puzzle. "*Mierda*. I mean, white bread and . . . I can't even tell what kind of meat this is. They want us to look perfect, work out, stay healthy . . . but they feed us slop out of a can and try to make it look like it belongs between two slices of bread."

"If we're lucky," replied Jesse. "That's why I'm just sticking with the fruit. It's the only thing here that looks even remotely fresh." She snapped the top of a banana and began to peel it. "Besides, this is the only place in the world I can eat one of these with one hand, without every guy in a five-block radius gawking."

Selina dropped her half-eaten lunch on a paper plate and pushed it away, toward the center of the kitchen table.

"I gotta start bringing my own," she said. Then, realizing that would mean less money to send home each month, she felt a twinge of guilt and reconsidered. She was just about to reach for her plate again when a freshly showered Brock approached the table in a pristine white terrycloth robe.

"Not gonna finish this?" he said, snatching the remnants from Selina's plate and pushing them between his lips. He said something else through a mouthful of food, but Selina couldn't understand what it was. Brock moved down to the other end of the table and took a seat.

A moment later, the only other male actor on set walked by, wearing nothing but a pair of loose red gym shorts and a tacky gold chain around his neck.

"Wow, you're still hungry, Jesse?" the actor said. "I figured you woulda been full from that big smoothie you just had back in the living room. Ha-ha. Although, I guess you got most of it on your tits, didn't you?"

"Shut the fuck up, Donald," said Selina.

"Hey. It's Dixon now. Dixon Kuntz."

The women giggled.

"Dixon Kuntz?" said Jesse.

"Great name, right?" Dixon asked, not expecting an answer. "Can't wait to see it in the credits of this piece of shit."

"Hey, where'd he get that?" asked Selina, looking across the room, pointing toward Peter. Peter sat on the floor off to the side, eating a massive sandwich on a long roll filled with all sorts of colorful meats and veggies. "Damn, that looks good."

"What? Who are you talking about?" asked Dixon, his train of thought shifting away from himself for a moment.

"Peter," said Jesse. "The PA."

"Oh, him. Yeah, he brings his own lunches. Smart kid," Dixon said. "You see his cooler over there? It says 'Lunch Box' on it, but I grabbed a marker and changed it to 'Munch Box'." Dixon burst into laughter. Selina and Jesse shot glances at each other.

"Munch Box," Dixon repeated to himself with a chuckle.

"Okay, everyone!" shouted Johnson, clapping his hands twice as he stood up from the lunch table. "Five minutes and we're at the pool out back. Brock, you're ready to go again, I assume? Selina, get whatever you need touched up touched up, and we'll see you for the anal scene on the diving board."

"Wait . . . *what?*" Selina said, taken off-guard. "That's Penelope's scene."

"Yeah, well, we had to make some script changes this morning," the director replied. "You may have noticed Miss Pujol's not here today."

"What are you talking about? Where is she, anyway?" Selina asked. Jesse looked up with the last bite of her banana between her teeth. She was just as confused as Selina.

"Shit, don't you chicks watch the news?" Dixon said. "Penelope was found dead last night, may her Pujol rest in peace."

"What?!" Selina's and Jesse's mouths dropped open in unison. The end of Jesse's banana hit the floor. "Dead? What happened?" they both asked.

"They don't know," said Johnson. "Someone found her body at that place we shot at the other day. Police said it looks like she choked to death on something, but they don't know what, or how exactly. Pretty weird shit."

Jesse and Selina looked at each other, their jaws still in their laps.

"Hey, uh," said Brock from the end of the table, "if you're not gonna eat the last piece of that banana . . . "

2

Foxy Roxoff sat in a booth in the corner of the bar, shaken. Her glass of wine sat untouched on the wooden table, her hands in her lap. She was leaning back in her seat with her head resting against the back of the booth, flattening the back of her afro.

She stared at the empty bench directly across from her, her eyes locked on the corner where the fake leather upholstery had given way to expose the yellow foam beneath. She kept her teeth clenched.

"There you are," said Jesse, approaching as if from nowhere. "Sorry we're late. Selina got roped into doing an extra scene."

"Yeah, sorry," said Selina. "You can bet I made sure that prick Johnson paid me for it up front, though. In cash. I squeezed an extra couple hundred out of him too. Of course, I'm the one paying for it now. *Mierda.*" She reached behind and rubbed the back pocket of her jeans. "I'm glad you got a booth."

"Yeah, I spent enough of the day on a hard wooden chair myself," said Jesse. "So . . . what's shakin', Foxy?"

Foxy didn't respond. Her posture didn't change. She didn't even realize her friends had joined her.

"*Hellooooo*," said Selina, waving a hand directly in front of Foxy's face. "Hey!"

"Oh . . . s-sorry . . ." Foxy finally snapped back to the present and sat up. "Sorry. Hi."

"What's up?" asked Jesse as she slid into the booth behind Selina. The bar was dimly lit, darker than it was outside.

"I had a shoot today," Foxy began, fixing her hair. She told them about how things had been set up through her old agent—a guy she had recently fired, when he attempted to get Foxy to pay him in blow jobs instead of his usual percentage. This had been the last shoot he set up for her, and she was anxious to just get it over with and move on. She only followed through with showing up because of her reputation. Some people didn't pay much respect to porn stars, but Foxy was a professional, goddammit.

"But when I got to the place," she continued, "there was no crew, no other actors or anything. I mean, the house looked like it was set up for a shoot. Lighting rigs and everything, and the bathroom was stocked. There was just . . . no one around."

A waitress appeared, and asked what Jesse and Selina would like.

"I'll have a Dark and Stormy," Selina said, telling herself one pricey drink was okay because she had made some good money today.

"Great. And you?"

"Oh, I need a beer," responded Jesse. "Whatever the darkest, strongest stout you have on tap is. Thanks."

"You got it," said the waitress. "Everything okay with your wine, hon?"

"Oh. Yeah," said Foxy, grabbing the glass and taking a sip to demonstrate.

"Oh! Also a shot of bourbon for me, please," Jesse said before turning her attention back to Foxy. "So then what?"

Foxy said she had looked around the house a bit and called out for anyone who might be lurking around, but there was no response. She poked her head into a few rooms, but it became pretty obvious no one else was there. It took her a moment to realize how nervous she suddenly was. Her heart was thumping in her chest.

Just then, a man's voice called out to her. "Is that you, Miss Roxoff?" he shouted.

She jumped, took a deep breath, then answered, "Yes, I'm here."

"Good, good. We'll be right with you. We're just tidying a few things up back here in the kitchen. Uh . . . Did you bring your test results?"

Foxy couldn't tell quite where the voice was coming from. There was a long hall ahead of her, with a number of doors off either side. "Yeah, I've got 'em right here. Where's the kitchen? I'll bring them to you."

"No, no!" the man shouted. It was a loud voice, the line it delivered bordering on anger. "I'll be . . . we'll be right with you in just a moment!"

"And at that point, something just kicked in," Foxy told her friends. "My adrenaline was pumping, and I got the hell outta there. He screamed something else at me when I hit the front door, but by then my heartbeat was pounding in my ears, and I just needed to leave. I was so creeped out."

"I don't blame you," Selina said. "Shit, if I roll up to a shoot and there's no one there to greet me at the door, I turn diva right off the bat."

"It got even worse. I guess the front door locked on its own when I came in, and the damn thing wouldn't open. I'm standing there fumbling with the lock, and the fuckin' guy jumps out into the hall yelling *'Get back here, bitch'*, and I'm like *'Hell no, motherfucker!'*"

"So you saw him?" Jesse asked. "Who was it? Anyone we know?"

"I didn't get a good look. He was dressed all in black, and he had a big hat on, and the light was behind him. Luckily, I flipped the lock just in time, and raced out. Jumped right in the car and hit the gas."

Foxy's hands were quivering. She reached for her glass and downed it quickly.

"Holy shit," Jesse said. Foxy raised her eyebrows and nodded, taking a deep breath.

"You hear about Penelope Pujol?" Foxy said. Her friends

nodded. "I've just been sitting here thinking, shit, that could've been me. I could be dead right now."

"I don't even want to think about that," Jesse said.

"Me neither," said Foxy. "Drinks are on me tonight." The waitress arrived with Jesse's and Selina's drinks just then.

"Cheers to that," Selina said, raising her drink in the air.

"We're gonna need another round," said Foxy, catching the waitress before she turned away. "And fast. It's been one of those days." Foxy smiled.

"Coming right up."

3

"You about ready to get out of here?"

"Yeah." Dina sat on a black leather office chair. "Just buckling the straps on these overly complicated heels, and I'm right behind you."

"Right behind me? *Ooooh, baby!*" Riley bounced her eyebrows with extreme sarcasm.

Riley Rieldall was new to the business, twenty-one years old, and relatively new in town. She and Dina had been getting along well recently, and for that she was happy. She had gotten to know a few other people in the industry—Jesse Jinx had become a sort of mentor—but she had a friendlier connection with Dina.

Riley and Dina were the last two to leave the set, a recently abandoned floor of an office building Tickled Pink Productions had rented for the week to use for shooting parts of at least a dozen features, plus a variety of miscellaneous office-themed scenes that would make their way online for subscribers to the company's *"Giving Her the Business"* stream.

"So you're doing a scene with Rod next week, aren't you?" asked Riley.

"Mr. Rod Almondjoy—the one and only," said Dina, referring to the new guy on the block, the one all the starlets were anxious to climb on top of. "Have you worked with him already?"

"Yeah. My first scene, actually. Super nice guy," Riley said. "And he's fucking *huuuge*. So be ready for that. And don't go anywhere near his nipples. He'll completely freak out."

"Heh . . . Thanks, I'll remember that," Dina said with a chuckle. Surely Rod would inform her of that himself before they did their scene together. She thought the warning from Riley was cute, though.

Dina finished assembling her shoes, then grabbed the strap to her bag and hoisted it over her shoulder.

The women started for the door of the office but stopped for a second at the reception area. Dina picked a piece of paper off the receptionist's desk and showed it to Riley.

"Lorem ipsum dolor sit amet . . . What the heck language is this?" Riley said.

"It's a prop," said Dina. "That's just dummy text. Like a placeholder."

"Oh. Weird."

"These must be old, though," Dina continued. "With HD cameras now, you can pretty much read anything that's on screen. Of course, nobody's going to be checking out stuff in the background of these kinds of movies. Let's go." Dina motioned for the door.

"Are we supposed to hit the lights?" asked Riley.

"Nah. There's a cleaning crew that should be coming through at some point. They'll take care of it."

The pair walked down the hall to the elevator, then rode eight floors down to the lobby, which was mostly made of glass. A pair of small palm trees flanked the main doors.

"Dammit," Dina said. "I left my nail polish in the bathroom. I gotta go grab it. It's that expensive shit with the glitter and the stuff from the bile ducts of anteaters or whatever."

"Oh, okay," said Riley, wondering if she should wait for her friend.

"You go ahead, though," said Dina. "I should pee anyway. My bladder's the size of a pistachio."

"You sure?"

"Of course I'm sure. I'm gonna be a few. Plus, we have that orgy thing in the morning, so you better go home and get your beauty rest!"

"Shit, I forgot about that," said Riley. "Guess I'm not drinking tonight!"

"Yeah, right," said Dina. "That's not what I heard. I may not have known you very long, my dear, but I know what a girl in love with Bloody Marys looks like."

Riley flashed a smile. "Alrighty then. Text me later so I know you got home safe?"

"Yes, Mommy," said Dina in a mocking tone, already in the

elevator. *"Bye-eeee!"*

Dina sat on a toilet on the eighth floor, staring down at her feet, admiring the tan of her skin against the tiny white tiles of the bathroom floor. Looking at her toes, however, she noticed that the expensive nail polish she had used on them earlier was already starting to chip. *Fucking anteaters,* she thought.

She heard the understated squeal of the restroom door open.

"Sorry—I'll be out of here in just a second," she said. "I know you're trying to clean up."

She pulled some toilet paper from the roll and bunched it up in her hand. Then the lights went out.

"Hey!" she yelled. "There's someone in here! Just give me a second, okay?"

No response.

"Hello?"

"Dina?" a voice in the darkness asked. It was a man. "Dina Deekupp?"

"Y-yes."

"As in 'These D-cups will get your . . . dick up'?" the voice asked.

A chill ran through Dina's body. She hadn't used that line in a while. She reached down into her jeans pocket to retrieve her phone.

"Yeah, that's me," she said. "Can I get a little privacy, please? And maybe you could turn the light back on, on your way out? I'll sign something for you if you want when I'm done."

The man chuckled. "Sorry. I'll wait for you outside," he said. The door opened and closed, but the asshole left the light off.

Dina texted Riley: *Wtf. Janitor just walked in on me in the bathroom.* She waited a minute, but got no immediate response. Another message: *Now sitting here in the dark, ugh. You leave yet?*

Dina flushed and let herself out of the stall, using the glow from her phone to light the way. She moved toward the sink first and grabbed the bag she had left beside it, then turned her phone toward the door. The phone's screen didn't give much light—just enough to make out basic shapes and objects. Dina knew the phone had a flashlight feature, but she hadn't bothered to figure out how to activate it yet. She'd only had the phone for three months now.

"Hello?" she called out, trying to ascertain whether or not the creep was waiting right outside the door for her or not.

She made her way toward the door, found the light switch, and flicked it. The man was standing there, still inside the bathroom, right beside the door.

He was dressed completely in black, wearing a long overcoat, leather gloves, and a large, floppy fedora.

Dina gasped as he lunged at her, ramming his palms straight into her breasts, knocking her backward a step, before she fell to the ground. The back of her head tapped the tile—enough to feel it, but not hard enough to do any real damage. In the process, Dina's phone slipped from her hand and slid across the floor before hitting the wall beneath the sink.

Dina tried to scream, but the fall had knocked the wind out of her. After a few seconds that felt like forever, she took in a huge breath and gasped again. She pressed herself up to a seated position with her forearms and tried to decipher the dark silhouette in front of her as waves of panic cascaded throughout her body. For some reason, she couldn't make out the guy's face.

"What the fuck?" was all she could get out before the man lunged at her again, knocking her back down to the floor a second time. The man's overcoat parted as he led with his knees and dropped down to straddle her around the ribcage. She swatted at him, but her efforts did little. She screamed, but it seemed no one else was anywhere nearby. She suddenly felt regret about only attending that single one-hour self-defense class and subsequently forgetting everything she was supposed to have learned.

She did feel lucky to have such large breasts, however—not that they were natural—keeping him back a bit. In the moment, they felt like some sort of barrier. Or maybe that was just an odd, fear-induced rationalization.

They didn't keep him back. He inched forward, grabbing Dina's wrists with his gloved hands to restrain her and pressing his thighs into her breasts until he was able to pull her arms down to her sides before throwing his legs over those too. She felt pain in her biceps as he did this. She bucked, trying to throw him off, but he was either too strong or too heavy. The most she was able to do was knock him slightly into the vanity. It was enough to shake her jar of nail polish off the edge to shatter on the floor beside them, creating a splash of glittery blue paint with what no one would ever know was anteater stuff mixed in. But that was it. Beyond that, she felt helpless.

She couldn't even scream anymore because he had shoved a rag deep into her mouth. She tried anyway, but it was a helpless, muffled sound. Tears began dripping from the corners of Dina's eyes, and her mascara began to run. Then she passed out.

Dina woke up moments later with a lump in her throat. Her tongue—everything in her mouth—felt cold. The silhouette of a man in a black overcoat and a large hat was still right there in front of her. And she still wasn't able to see his face. *Had this guy managed to stay backlit this entire time? Was he wearing a mask?* She couldn't tell.

And that's when she realized she couldn't breathe either. The lump in her throat—there was something in there. The man was holding something against her mouth. He was choking her.

Dina bucked again, filled with more panic than before. She tried to twist herself free, but the man stayed heavy on top of her, keeping her where he wanted. She was able to shift slightly to one side, but he adjusted and kept her down. In the process, Dina felt something touch her left hand beneath the sink. Even with a black glove held firmly across her face she was able to turn just enough to see it was her phone. Her eyes widened. She still had a chance.

He seemed to be getting heavier, though. And the sound of blood throbbing in her ears was getting louder.

With her left thumb, she managed to type one more quick message to Riley. She hit "Send" as her vision blurred and the pressure in her throat became unbearable. It was only a few more seconds before everything went black.

4

Johnson Grande was kind of an asshole. He knew it. He knew other people knew it. He just didn't care. He was out for himself, and that was that. If anyone else got in his way, fuck 'em.

Unlike a lot of other porn directors, he hadn't gotten into the business through acting.

Huh—acting, he thought. Most of these idiots were barely elementary school-level thespians. Not that it was really about acting skills. This wasn't exactly Shakespeare. Or Broadway. Or Hollywood. He made fuck films with sexy bodies. It didn't matter to him, or to most people, whether or not they could act. As long as they looked good swapping fluids.

He had sort of stumbled into the directing thing, mainly because he had a working camcorder and a friend with a seriously hot wife who was looking to get into the industry. Next thing he knew, he was getting offers to shoot features on a weekly basis, while the friend and his wife broke up and both left town.

The money was okay back then. It was better now. And he'd been doing this for a while, so he was able to demand a bigger cut of anything he worked on. His name on a film meant something to the people who bought them.

His name meant something else entirely to the people who worked for him.

That didn't bother him too much, though. He kind of liked being feared, being hated. That's what Johnson really got off on.

He fell asleep that night thinking of ways he could twist his actors' limbs that would look good on camera while causing them a fair amount of pain and discomfort. That bitch Jesse in particular. He didn't like the way she spoke to him the other day.

5

Riley Rieldall woke up in a panic.

She shouldn't have gone out. She should have gone straight home, to bed. Instead, when she left Dina, she went to meet a friend at a bar and had a few too many drinks, then ended up walking home as the sun was coming up. That was just a couple hours ago.

She cursed herself for being irresponsible, for not acting like a goddamned grownup.

Upon arriving home, she had passed out on her couch. Now she was late for a shoot.

Riley raced to the bathroom, jumped in the shower, and ran a razor over everything. She'd call Johnson from the car and come up with some sort of excuse—something about traffic—and hope he hadn't already started to film anything without her. Maybe someone else would be running late too.

She threw on a tank top and jeans, grabbed her make-up bag and keys, and dashed out the door.

Riley wanted to be a star. But she knew she had to pull her head out of her ass if that was going to happen. The ones who make it, make it because they work hard. They act like professionals. They don't go out partying when they have to be on set at nine o'fucking-clock the next morning, ready to look sexy and fuck like they invented it.

Who the hell schedules an orgy for nine in the morning anyway? Especially an all-girl orgy with a dumb title like *Cum to My Window.* Johnson Grande, that's who. The prick. He wasn't answering his phone.

She stopped for a red light and noticed she had several unread text messages, all from Dina. No time to read them now, though. She'd just talk to her when she arrived at the shoot.

Riley pulled up to the location, a huge mansion in the Hills. It had a topiary garden out front and a cul-de-sac driveway packed with convertibles and vans. She had to park on the street, down the hill, what felt like a mile away from the front door. She grabbed her things and jogged up to the house. She spotted a PA, a guy she had seen before, carrying a lighting rig and a blue cooler with the words "Munch Box" scrawled on it in black marker.

"Hey!" she called out to him. "Peter, right?" He stopped and turned back.

"Yeah. Hi, Riley."

"Please tell me they haven't started yet," she said.

"I don't know, actually," he said. "I just got here myself. They can't have gotten too far into things without this rig, though."

"Okay, good." So she wasn't the only one. As long as Peter was a gentleman and let her enter the house first, she wouldn't technically be the last to arrive.

"Well, well," said Johnson, a bit louder than Riley would have liked. He was wearing a gaudy, colorful Hawaiian shirt, unbuttoned, the salt and pepper hair on his chest on full display. "Look who decided to join us."

Riley looked around the room. A dozen actresses were lounging on couches in robes, all looking tired, or bored, or both.

"Sorry, John. I tried to call," she said, huffing from her trip up the hill to the house.

The director turned away from her as Riley retrieved her phone from her pocket.

"Okay, we're just waiting on one more girl and then we can get things rolling," Johnson announced, as he left the living room for the kitchen, which had been transformed into a makeshift make-up area. "Has anyone heard from Dina Deekupp?"

Johnson's question jolted Riley. *Dina wasn't there yet?*

"Hey, hon. Rough night?" It was H.R. Gagger, star of the *Trucker Fuckers* series. Riley hadn't noticed him when she came in. "What's wrong? You look like you've seen a ghost all of a sudden."

"Dina's not here?" she said. "I . . . I just saw her last night."

"No, nobody's heard from her so far. A few of us have tried calling and texting, but no response."

"Yeah, I just saw these texts she sent me last night . . . I hope she's okay."

"I'm sure she's fine," Gagger said. "Hopefully she's on her way, though. John's starting to get pissed."

"Yeah, I hope so too," said Riley. "These texts . . . " She handed her phone over.

"Oh shit," Gagger said. "Guess someone had a peeper. Like I said, though, I'm sure she's fine. She's a tough cookie. What's this last one, though? You girls have some kind of code or something."

Riley took the phone back and focused on the last message. It was just one word: *Fedora.*

"Not a clue," she said. "She was going to text me when she got home. I guess it's an autocorrect thing." Riley slipped the phone into her pocket.

"Hmm. Well, let's get you to make-up, honey," Gagger said. "Not that you don't wake up gorgeous."

"Wait a second," Riley said. "*Why are you even here?* It just dawned on me."

"I dunno. Something goofy in the script. It's a paycheck."

"Mmm, I'd love to go for a ride on that," said Jesse, admiring H.R. Gagger from across the living room. He was a near-perfect specimen as far as she was concerned, standing about 6'3" and packed with muscle, both arms tattooed with colorful Japanese sleeves, his chest covered with beautiful black hair. "You ever work with him?"

"Nah," said Foxy. "I wish. He's on the other team, so to speak." She massaged her temples. "Damn, my head hurts."

"Like, for real, you mean?" Jesse couldn't believe it. "I always thought he was gay-for-pay."

"Nope. He's the real deal. Those *Cummy Bears* movies? Totally his idea. He's just here so we can look at him and get frustrated."

"Fuck," said Jesse, staring at his abs.

Selina returned from make-up and fell into the couch between Foxy and Jesse. "*Cabron.* I can't believe this. I have glitter in my eyes already. I told that asshole . . ."

"Wait, so why is he here, then?" asked Jesse.

"Gagger?" asked Selina, joining in the conversation. "I know, right? Mel said it's a joke thing. Guess he's going to jerk off on the drapes or something."

"Damn," Jesse whispered. "Hmm . . . I wonder if I can catch his eye and maybe convince him to do straight-for-pay. Even if it's just for today. Or tonight, at my apartment."

Foxy laughed. "Good luck! Umm, I guess you haven't seen *Cummy Bears,* huh? He *reeeeeeally* likes dick. Almost as much as you do."

"We'll see," Jesse said with a smile. "Let me know if you want to put some money on it."

"Hey now," said Selina. "Don't go throwing money away. You start gambling on sure losses and you'll never get Jinx Pix off the ground."

Jesse took a deep breath and sighed. "I know. But just look at him."

"Well, Dina's boyfriend just called," announced Johnson. "She's sick. Said she ate something last night that didn't agree with her. So we're officially one slut short of a legitimate lez-fest here. Anyone have any hot friends looking to make a few hundred bucks? Preferably someone nearby? Anyone have Keiko's number?"

Riley twisted her brow. Jesse was standing beside her.

"You doing okay, hon?" she asked. "You look a little hungover."

"Huh? Oh . . . yeah, I'm fine," said Riley. "It's just, I don't think Dina has a boyfriend."

"Really?"

"Yeah. I mean, we're not exactly besties, but as far as I know, she's single. I dunno . . . Something doesn't seem right. We did a shoot together last night, and then I got all these texts from her, and now she's a no-show." Riley pulled up the text conversation and handed the phone to Jesse.

"Yeah, this is all a little weird. I don't like it. First Penelope turns up dead, and now this. I think I'm gonna talk to the cops. You want to come with?"

"Okay, people," said Johnson to the group. He paused a second to let the conversations in the room die down a bit. "We're just going to move forward and get this fuck-show on the road.

Riley, I want you and Foxy on the couch, bent over the arms on either side. Selina, I need you on your knees on the coffee table. Caitlin, Heidi, I'll be with you both in a minute. Jesse, follow me. I've got something special I need you to wear."

6

"And what the fuck was that outfit all about?" Riley pulled into the parking lot of the police station. "Johnson really seems to have it in for you, huh?"

"Yeah, he didn't like that I asked for a pillow at our last shoot," said Jesse. "Apparently he doesn't like my tattoos either. Guess he decided to take out his frustrations in the form of whatever the fuck that thing was."

It had been something along the lines of a way-too-tight bodysuit, made up of a series of criss-crossing black rubber straps with dildos sprouting from each intersection. The rubber cowl had a dildo protruding from each of Jesse's ears too, and at one point, two other women had to back themselves up against the sex-helmet.

"Sorry if I slammed into your head too hard," Riley said. "I was trying to gauge Heidi's rhythm and match it, but that chick's so coked out all the time, it wasn't easy."

"Oh, I'm fine. The little hard rubber nubs on the inside were the worst part. I've got these red polka dots all over me."

"Oh shit, I didn't even notice that," said Riley.

"Yeah. Well, at least I've got matching bruises on both sides of me now," said Jesse, lifting the side of her t-shirt up and rubbing the inked skin along her ribs. "It's good to be able to breathe again, though."

"The rubber shoes were kinda cute," said Riley. "But I'm glad he didn't ask anyone to insert the heels."

Riley parked and turned off the ignition.

"Hey, before we head in," she said, "I just wanted to let you know how much I appreciate you."

"Appreciate me?" Jesse said. "Hey, I'm concerned about Dina too. I didn't feel right having you come over here all by yourself."

"No, I mean, in general. I mean, all the advice you've given me about the business. Not to mention hooking me up with that killer apartment. Just, you know, everything."

"Aww, that's sweet, honey." Jesse was touched by the sentiment. Riley reminded Jesse of herself when she first started in the industry. She was happy to look out for the younger girls coming up and wanted to make sure they didn't make the same mistakes she had made early on. That was another reason she wanted to start her own thing. The fewer people being taken advantage of, the better.

"Yeah, I just wanted to let you know," Riley said. "You're

kind of my hero."

Jesse laughed.

"Well, let's not get carried away," she said.

"No, I mean it. Jinx Pix is going to be awesome. It's nice to know there are some smart people in this business. I was just talking to my folks the other night, telling them how you've helped me kind of navigate things out here."

"That's great that your parents are so supportive," Jesse said. "I definitely never had that."

"Well, yeah, they don't exactly like it," Riley said. "But they respect me enough to let me make my own decisions. Plus, the business has a stigma, but it's nothing like what it used to be."

"True," said Jesse. "Well, you ready to head in and talk to some cops?"

"Not exactly how I envisioned my day going, but yeah, let's do it."

"And what makes you think she was murdered?" asked Officer Knowles. He leaned back in his chair and began to tap the end of a pen lightly on his thigh.

"We *don't* know that," said Jesse from the opposite side of the desk. "That's why we're here. We know she's missing, and someone else we know was found dead recently, so we're scared."

"We were working together last night," said Riley, handing the officer her phone. "Later on, she sent me these texts. Something just seems off, you know?"

Knowles looked at the phone but didn't respond right away.

"She didn't show up for work this morning," said Jesse. "Before we came here, we went to the place where yesterday's shoot was, but we couldn't get in. Then we went to her apartment. Nothing. She's not home. Her neighbor said she hadn't seen her since yesterday morning, and her car's been gone the whole time. It's like she just vanished after sending those texts."

"Hmmm. So when you say you two were 'working together', Miss Rieldall, you mean the two of you were, uh . . ."

"Look," interrupted Jesse, "is there, like, some way we can track her phone or something? Or can you at least go to that office building and see if she's still there?"

"You sure she wasn't on drugs?" asked Knowles. "Maybe she OD'd." The officer brought the end of his pen up toward his mouth and tapped his lower lip with it.

"No, she isn't on drugs," said Riley. "She's been clean for years."

"And *we're* not on drugs, either," said Jesse, anticipating Knowles' next question. The tension in the conversation was rising quickly. It was obvious what Knowles thought of them, and Jesse was getting annoyed.

"Yeah, okay," Knowles continued. "So you two leave your little porno movie shoot last night, and oops, your friend forgets something, so she heads back inside. She starts sending you crazy messages a little while later. Are you really sure she didn't go back in to take a couple hits of something? Maybe she does a few bumps of coke, huh? Or shoots something weird into her arm. Maybe it makes her a little nuts. She starts texting nonsense,

39

maybe takes more drugs . . ."

"And what about the word 'fedora'?" Jesse said. "You don't think that could be some sort of clue?"

"A clue?! Your friend got high and started texting nonsense. Either that, or she was so blitzed, she couldn't see the letters on the screen, and her autocorrect thought she was talking about a hat." Knowles paused a second, and sat up in his chair, placing his elbows on the desk.

"Do me a favor, and think about something. How well did you really know your friend? Hmm? Were you really that close? Or were you just a bunch of sluts who screwed the same handful of guys over and over for money?"

Riley and Jesse both gritted their teeth, furious at their treatment by the officer. No one else at the precinct had been much help either. This felt like a dead end.

"As far as I'm concerned, there's nothing left to talk about here," Knowles said. "I'm real sorry your friend's missing, but you all have a pretty dangerous line of work in common. I suggest you look for some other form of employment."

"So that's it then?" Jesse said. "Can't we at least file a Missing Persons Report?"

"That's not how things work here. Sorry, girls." Knowles stood up from the desk. He placed his pen in his shirt pocket, then collected a few scattered sheets of paper from the desk and jogged them together.

"'Sorry'? That's all?" said Jesse, raising her palms up. Knowles ignored her.

"Come on, let's go," said Riley, touching Jesse on the elbow. "This is pointless." The women stood up from their chairs.

On the way out, Jesse stopped in the doorway and turned back. "What was your first name again, officer?"

"Richard."

"Huh," Jesse said. "You seem more like a *Dick* to me."

7

Anita Kochnow rubbed the knot in her neck with one hand as she tried to pull her thong back on with the other. It didn't help that the driver of the van seemed to be making a game out of hitting every pothole in the city.

"Damn, when I signed up for this shit, I figured you had some kind of staging area or something," she said, annoyed. "Even if it was just a tent or something. I didn't know I'd have to clean up with a roll of paper towels and get dressed while we were still moving."

"*Minivan MILFs*," said Woodley, her one-named director/co-star for the afternoon. "One hundred percent real, just like the website says. *We pick you up, you suck us off.*"

"Yeah, well, if I was just here to suck you off, why'd I have to be completely nude?"

"Don't be stupid, Anita. You do realize what the fuck this is, right?" Woodley was growing more perturbed with each passing block. The driver hit another pothole, and Woodley and Anita both fell sideways, slamming their heads into the tinted window on the side door. "*Yo, see if you can get us off Swiss Cheese Ave, will ya?*"

The driver didn't respond. He had trained himself to keep quiet during these minivan shoots and focus himself completely on not getting into collisions and not drawing the attention of any cops. That sometimes meant driving down less-travelled streets and unkempt access roads. He made a turn.

Anita winced and rubbed the top of her head, then righted herself and finished getting dressed as best she could.

"Your neck okay?" Woodley asked. "I mean, I hope I didn't stab your throat too hard with this thing." He pointed to his now flaccid penis, still wet with Anita's saliva, as if she didn't know what he was referring to. She didn't bother to answer him.

"Anyway, like I was sayin'," Woodley continued, "we pick you up, you suck us off. Then we drop your ass off. And your stop's up here." Still nude, he grabbed his jeans off the seat and extracted a wad of crumpled cash from the pocket. He tossed it at Anita, who made no attempt to catch it as it hit her stomach and fell to the floor.

"You're a disrespectful prick," she said, her eyes locked on Woodley. He broke the stare and reached behind the back seat.

"Don't worry. It's all there." His hand returned from behind the seat with something wrapped in silver foil. "Oh, and I almost forgot. We did promise you a meal. So here's your complimentary *Minivan MILFs* hot dog. Enjoy." He held the foil-wrapped meal forward, offering it to Anita.

"Fuck you," she said. "And fuck your hot dog too."

The driver stopped, and the side door of the van slid open automatically.

"Thanks for today, Anita," Woodley said. "Hopefully we can do it again in a few months."

"You're seriously kicking me out *here*?" she said, now even more annoyed. The area was an unfamiliar grid of warehouses, most of which appeared to be abandoned and to have fallen into disrepair.

"Well, yeah. I mean, we're headed north, and you live in the Valley, right?" Woodley said. "Plus, we're late, so . . . ya know . . . thanks again."

"I don't even know where we are," Anita said, looking around at what seemed to be a collection of concrete boxes with shattered windows.

"So take the hot dog and see if you can trade it to a homeless guy for directions. Listen, we gotta roll, so please get out of the fucking van."

Anita just stared at Woodley. So he gave her a nudge on the shoulder. Then he grabbed both of her shoulders and threw her out of the vehicle. With only one of her heels on, she stumbled and fell. Woodley tossed the other shoe out the door.

He yelled, "Thank you very MILF!" as the door closed and the van sped off, kicking up a cloud of dirt and loose gravel.

"Asshole!" she yelled at the back of the rapidly shrinking van.

Then she laughed. "MILF," she said, quieter, to herself. *"I'm fucking thirty."*

Anita pulled herself up off the street and strapped her second heel on. She brushed the dirt off her skirt, then gave her sore neck another squeeze. She looked up, trying to identify some of the skyscrapers in the distance, trying to figure out exactly where she was, and which direction it made the most sense to travel. Dusk was setting in, so she knew she'd better figure it out soon.

She heard the soft sizzle of tires on pavement from around the corner and felt a sudden sense of relief. Maybe Woodley wasn't quite as much of an asshole as she thought. Maybe the mounted cameras in the van were still going that whole time and it was just part of the shtick for the site. She hadn't bothered watching any *Minivan MILFs* videos before agreeing to the shoot. Rookie mistake.

She figured the van would roll around the corner any second and Woodley would greet her with a smile and a hug and explain everything. She'd most likely forgive him. After all, it wasn't the first time she'd been treated like shit on a shoot. And it surely wouldn't be the last. But what was she going to do? Go back to school? You needed money for that, and she never seemed to have enough. Which was exactly the reason she agreed to do things like blow some stranger in a minivan and let him film it and put it online for a few hundred dollars. Eventually, she hoped, she'd make a name for herself. Maybe the video she just shot would be the one people would notice. Maybe it would be the one to break her. Suddenly she'd be in demand, and the money would roll in.

She just had to keep pushing. But time was running out. As she'd just said out loud to herself, *she was thirty years old.*

A car—not a van—rolled slowly around the corner, and Anita's heart sank. Not that she was entirely surprised. Dashed hopes she could cope with. For a little longer, at least.

The car pulled up alongside her and stopped. There was a short pause before the passenger-side window lowered. The man inside asked if she needed help or a ride somewhere.

Anita hesitated. Accepting rides from strangers was, of course, rarely a good idea. But she wasn't even completely sure where she was. Maybe the driver could drop her off near the library. She could catch a bus home from there. In the meantime, she figured she could defend herself.

Anita got in the car, and the man started driving. He offered her a bottle of water, which she accepted.

Anita woke up inside one of the abandoned buildings. It was dark. She was groggy, but had enough of her wits to realize what had happened.

The flick of a wooden match sounded from ten feet away. The man from the car was sitting in a beat-up office chair on wheels. The leather appeared to have been stripped from it, leaving only the metal frame and some foam cushioning. He lit a candle and stood it on the cement floor, securing it by first letting a few drops of molten wax fall.

He was wearing a dark overcoat and a hat. Anita hadn't been able to see much of his face in the car, especially since the interior light hadn't come on when she opened the door. She wasn't able to see any of it now. *Was he wearing some sort of a mask?*

"Now, now, Miss Kochnow," the man said. "Even in the low light, I can see the panic in your eyes. No need for that."

Anita tried to stand, but quickly realized she had been restrained. Her wrists were bound with one length of rope, her ankles with another. A third piece of rope circled both her abdomen and one of the support columns in the room.

The knot in her neck was still there too.

"Of course, there's no need for you to be a filthy whore either," the man continued. "But that hasn't stopped you."

The man stood up from the chair and moved into one of the darker corners of the space. His shoes crunched on the filth that had accumulated on the floor over the years. Anita wondered when the building had last had a tenant.

"What do you want?" she asked, frightened.

The man didn't respond, but she heard him fumbling with something in the darkness. Soon, he was moving again, but he managed to only walk along the edges of the room, where she couldn't see him.

"What do you want from me?" she repeated. "Are you looking for money? I'm broke, but you can have what I've got on me."

"I'm more concerned with what's been going in you," the man said from somewhere behind her. A new layer of fear shot

SCOTT COLE

through Anita.

"Why choose this way of life, Miss Kochnow? Why be such a terrible, awful person? Don't you know the damage you've been causing?"

Before Anita could respond, something whizzed past the left side of her head. A hand. A black leather glove grabbed her forehead and pulled backward, bracing her head against the column. She struggled, but it was pointless.

"I know what you were doing in that van," the man said. "This should feel familiar."

Another hand appeared to her right. It held something. Something large. She could feel cold air. Then her lips went numb as the man placed the object against them, and pressed toward her mouth.

Anita's lips were forcibly parted, and something hard tapped her front teeth. Soon, her entire mouth was cold. The man tilted her head around the column and back further. Then her throat filled with the same sensation of cold. *Brainfreeze*, she thought, as an intense headache took hold fast and she experienced a flash of her childhood: devouring a push-up pop from the ice cream man on a hot summer day, and doing so far too quickly.

A minute later, the cylinder of ice had clogged her throat. Anita had been known for her ability to deep throat some of the industry's "biggest" stars, but this was too much for her to handle. Breathe through your nose, she told herself. Easier said than done when you're being attacked. She thought for a second that if she could just stay calm and hold on for a few more seconds, maybe enough ice would melt to clear a narrow path for air.

Then the hand on her forehead let go, and for a second, Anita thought she had a chance. But she wasn't even able to tip her head forward with the ice in her throat.

The man pinched Anita's nose tight.

In the last moments of her life, Anita Kochnow saw the flicker of a candle's flame, but felt cold. It all seemed so strange.

8

"Here we are, ladies. One chocolate and one vanilla."

Foxy and Jesse shot glances at each other and resisted the urge to burst into laughter as the server set the milkshakes down, placing the chocolate in front of Foxy and the vanilla in front of Jesse. When he left, they lost it, but still waited a minute before swapping glasses, not wanting to correct the waiter's mistake in front of him.

The ice cream shop was a place Jesse loved but didn't visit very often. It had been a rough week, though, so she was allowing herself a treat.

"Did I ever tell you the name I almost went with?" asked Foxy.

Jesse shook her head as she pulled a mouthful of dessert through her old-timey paper straw.

"*Foxy Browneye.* Like the movie . . . sort of. Can you believe that shit?"

Jesse's eyes went wide for a split-second, then closed abruptly as she snorted, inhaling some of her milkshake before blowing twin bubbles of chocolate liquid out her nose.

"See? I knew I could teach you how to squirt!" Foxy said, delighted by Jesse's reaction. She pulled a handful of paper napkins from the dispenser on the table and handed them over to Jesse, whose eyes were still closed and now dripping tears. A thread of drool had escaped the corner of her mouth as well. She sat there, laughing silently, as she cleaned herself up.

"I mean, I was just so, so ready for a change," Foxy continued. "Law turned out not to be anywhere near as exciting as I had hoped when I was in school," Foxy continued. "I guess I was kind of lashing out against my own life up to that point."

Jesse regained her composure and placed a couple wads of milkshake-saturated napkins on the table. "Yeah, Roxoff is, like, a billion times better."

"You know, we shouldn't even be having these," Foxy said. "We have that shoot with the Rods on Thursday."

"You're right, as usual," said Jesse. "But I kinda don't care. When Jinx Pix is up and running, I'll be open to all of it. Skinny, fat, tall, short, gay, straight, body-modded, androgynous, hair-diapered, whatever. There's someone out there looking for anything and everything you can think of."

"Well, in the meantime, we're gonna have to deal with the wrath of Al Dente if we're not in perfect shape on shoot day," said Foxy.

"Yeah, I'll be hitting the gym later if you want to join me. I don't know who's worse—Al or Johnson."

"They're both assholes," said Foxy. "Just, like, two different flavors of asshole."

Jesse puckered her lips and squeezed a drop of her milkshake out, letting it fall back into her glass.

Foxy made a disgusted face and a sound to go with it.

"You're nasty," she said, shaking her head. "Anyway, not to bring the conversation down or anything, but, uh . . . you see the news?"

Jesse looked puzzled and shook her head no while taking another sip of her shake.

"Missy Mounds," Foxy said. "Dead."

"What?! Missy Mounds? Like, from the plus-size *300* parody?"

"They found her this morning in a hotel room," said Foxy. "It was registered under a fake name and paid for in cash. Of course, they're saying it was drugs, but that sounds like some bullshit to me."

"Holy shit," said Jesse. "Did you know her?"

"A little. Not well. But well enough to know she never touched drugs in her life."

"Yeah, you know, when Riley and I went to the cops about Dina, the officer just kept going on about how she probably OD'd somewhere. But she had been clean forever."

"Something's up," said Foxy. "Penelope, Dina, and now Missy. And supposedly Anita Kochnow's been MIA for a few days too. Not to mention my little run-in the other day. This can't be random."

"It's fucking scary," Jesse said. "We need to do something."

"Of course. But what can we do?"

"Rod? Hi, I'm Jesse. I guess we're working together today." She was wearing jeans and a tight t-shirt emblazoned with the words "Cum On My Tats".

Rod Almondjoy removed his feet from the arm of the love seat, and stood up, flipping his copy of *Vaginaficionado* closed.

"Hey Jesse," he said, dropping the magazine onto the coffee table. He reached an open hand out, and Jesse shook it. Then they gave each other a quick introductory hug. "Nice to finally meet you. You were amazing in *Yo-Ho-Ho and a Bucket of Cum.*"

"Oh, thanks," she said, rolling her eyes, silently recalling the hell of that shoot and how the director had forced her to keep her right leg folded and bound the entire time so they could attach a wooden peg-leg to her knee. She kept wondering how that was going to work during her sex scenes, but the director had somehow managed to shoot around the fact she did indeed have two complete, working legs.

Jesse pointed to Rod's magazine. "Is that the new issue? I haven't seen it yet."

"Yeah, it just came out," Rod said. "I like to, uh, *stay on top of things.*"

"Well, we'll get to that soon, right?" Jesse said with a smile. "But remember, I like to be on top too." Jesse let her joke linger for a second, then continued. "So . . . any don'ts?"

"My nipples are hyper-sensitive, so as long as you stay away from them, we're good. You?"

"No choking and no slapping above the neck. Otherwise I'm up for whatever," Jesse said. "I'll see you in a bit. I have to run over to make-up."

"Ah, 'Happy' Mel," Rod said. "Good luck."

"I don't know why you ladies degrade yourselves like this," Mel said. "Wouldn't you rather get yourselves more respectable jobs?"

Mel felt a twinge of guilt in her words. After all, it had never been her dream to do make-up for the porn industry. She had always wanted to work in mainstream Hollywood, or at the very least, open her own salon. But the competition for work at the big studios was pretty fierce, with too many people vying to make the same dreams come true. So she settled for this. It was still the movie business, after all. And the pay was good. Just not good enough for her to keep her trap shut all the time.

Her demeanor had earned her the nickname "Happy" from the

actors she prepped before they went off to screw each other senseless. She was aware of the name, even if it was never spoken to her directly. She didn't care. A job was a job. At least she was able to practice her art, even if it was in a morally reprehensible field.

"Yeah, I tried that 'respectable job' thing already," said Foxy, anxious to get out of the chair. "I used to practice law."

Mel was a bit startled by the response, and momentarily stopped the flow of the airbrush. "Really?" she asked, genuinely curious. "What . . . what happened?"

"It just didn't take," Foxy said. "Besides, most days, this is a hell of a lot more fun. Sex is great, Mel. You should try it sometime. We finished here?"

Mel looked at Foxy head on, piercing her for a moment with her stare, then sprayed one last burst of blush across Foxy's cheek.

"We are now," Mel said.

Foxy popped up from her chair and looked in the mirror, patting the right side of her afro softly. "You do nice work, Mel," she said. "Too bad you're not a little more open-minded." Foxy air-kissed her reflection, then walked away before Mel had a chance to respond.

On her way to the living room, Foxy passed Jesse in the hallway.

"Well, I found my Rod," Jesse said. "Where's yours?"

"Fuck if I know," Foxy said. "I went straight to make-up."

"Oh, that's where I'm headed now."

"Have fun," said Foxy, twisting her lips to the side of her face. Jesse acknowledged the look, and Foxy wished her luck as they continued on their separate paths.

A man rounded the corner suddenly.

"Looking for a long shaft?" he blurted out. Foxy jumped, making a squeak. It was Dixon Kuntz. He struck a pose, leaning into the wall with his shoulder, and gestured toward his crotch with an open hand, like a model offering a new product up for display.

"No thanks, Donald," Foxy said, rolling her eyes. "I've got a date for the afternoon already." She tried to push past him, but Dixon blocked her path.

"Yeah, see, that's what I was about to tell you," Dixon said. "Rod Longshaft called out sick. Some bad fish or something. So they called me in from the bullpen."

"Wait . . . what?"

"As fate would have it," he continued with a smile, "you and I are working together today."

Foxy's stomach did a flip. She managed to keep her lunch down, but she wasn't sure how long that would last.

"That was vile," Foxy said, unlocking the doors to her car.

Jesse just laughed as she got in on the passenger side. She couldn't stop.

"That was the most disgusting thing I've ever done. That was . . . gross. Just gross. I don't know what else to say about it."

"Well you played it off pretty well in the moment," Jesse said, still unable to control her laughter. "I mean, that was some top-shelf hate-fucking if you ask me. Good thing that's what the sce-ne called for, or Al would've been pissed."

"I wouldn't have been able to go through with it otherwise. I mean, could you smell his balls from where you were standing? I almost threw up. Ugh ... " Foxy gagged on the end of her words, then covered her mouth with the back of a hand. "Gross. So gross."

"That reminds me," Jesse said. "You want to run to the store with me? I need to pick up some brie."

"Stop," said Foxy, with a dry-heave. "I'm gonna puke right here in the car."

"I liked the way you dodged his pop shot too." Jesse chuckled again. "You're just like, *'Okay, I'm outta here! Clean-up in aisle five!'*" Jesse burst into full-on laughter again, while Foxy just shook her head, trying to keep herself composed and focused on driving.

"So gross," she repeated.

"Anyway," Jesse said. "We've all been there. But, you know ... Jinx Pix ... We're not gonna need to do that shit any more. I'm gonna run things the way they ought to be run."

"Well hit the lottery or something quick, then, okay? If I get stuck working with that stinky cheese-dick again, I might actu-ally break the damn thing off."

The sun was just beginning to set, turning the sky into smears of orange and pink.

"So, uh ... where was Riley?" asked Foxy. "I thought she was supposed to be there today."

"No, she went home to visit her parents," Jesse said. "Her parents, who totally support what she does, by the way."

"That's amazing," Foxy said. "Hey, you want to grab a drink? I brushed before we left, but I could use a shot or two to sanitize my mouth."

"Can't," said Jesse, with a smile.

"You can't? How come? Hot date?"

"Maaaybe."

"What do you mean 'maybe'?"

Jesse's smile grew wider. "Gagger's cooking me dinner tonight. I'm supposed to be at his place at eight."

"What? Gagger?"

"Yeah, we've been talking."

"Girl, do you not pay attention to the things I say?" Foxy shook her head. Jesse's smile faded slightly. *The man is gay!*

"Yeah, yeah. Don't believe everything you see in the movies."

"I'm talking truth, honey," said Foxy. "Listen, I'm sure if you go over there, you'll get a delicious home-cooked meal. But it's not going to be the kielbasa you're looking for. You should probably just stay home and watch one of the *Cummy Bears* movies—there are seventeen of them, by the way—and face the facts."

Jesse kept smiling. She couldn't not smile.

"We'll see," she said.

10

Selina was lounging on a crushed velvet couch inside a gigantic, secluded house in the Hills. The wallpaper was ornate, the furniture looked antique, and everything that could be gold, was. She hadn't seen much of the place yet, but the room she was in was stunning.

She imagined she would soon be wearing more jewelry than she had ever seen in her life and getting slammed from behind by someone playing the part of an aristocrat with a huge cock and a penchant for brown girls. Maybe they'd be wearing powdered wigs or something equally silly. She loved her job.

Her old friend Ana had gotten her this gig. Ana was going by the name Anya now. Anya Lapp. She had moved to Europe for a few years (Selina couldn't remember where exactly), and starred in a number of very popular softcore films dubbed *The Eurotica Diaries*. Now she was back in the States, doing the occasional porn shoot between regularly scheduled webcam sessions. She seemed to be very well-connected and had apparently slid right into the scene almost immediately upon her return home.

The two of them had been out of touch for a while. But recently Selina had been trying to make some extra money here and there, and it turned out Anya had a hookup. She figured she'd do the shoot, and then they'd go out for a drink and get caught up.

Just one drink, though. She didn't want to piss all her money away. Not that her bank account was hurting, exactly. She was just doing her best to send a little more than usual home each month.

Her parents lived in Mexico, having been deported years ago, thanks to a tip from some unemployed "good ol' boy" and a politician trying to make a name for himself. The only stroke of luck in the whole mess was the fact Selina had been born in the US, and was therefore a citizen and allowed to stay.

Her parents agreed Selina would have far more opportunities staying in the US. But they probably never dreamed she would go into porn.

Selina Southgate certainly had a fan base, though she had never been a top name. Southgate, of course, wasn't her real name either. Just another porn pun.

She looked forward to the day Jesse got Jinx Pix up and running, with her promises of higher percentages for performers, along with more say in virtually everything. But until that day, she danced at clubs and gave lap dances to horny strangers and did extra porn shoots whenever she could score them.

Anya had met her at the beautiful, gilded door to the enormous home.

"I love these houses," she had said. "I can't believe the owners rent them out for this sort of thing."

"So where is everyone?" Selina asked into the open air. Anya had greeted her, then asked Selina to have a seat and wait for the director, whom she would go fetch. But ten minutes had passed since then, and Selina hadn't seen or heard anyone in that time. She wondered what was taking so long.

"Anya?" she called out. "Where'd you run off to?" There was no response beyond the echo of her own voice as it travelled down the cavernous hall.

After calling out a few more times with the same result, Selina decided to go exploring. She grabbed her bag off the floor and threw the strap over her shoulder. The thing was heavy. It reminded her of an old boyfriend who used to joke she must be a boxer to want to deal with such a heavy bag all the time.

"Hellooooo?" she said, practically yelling. Nothing.

The hallway was dark, but she could see light down at the end of it. Anya had to be there. Maybe she had gotten sidetracked by a conversation with the director, or one of their co-stars. Or maybe she got pinned down to the make-up chair and no one realized they had to come back and get Selina.

She passed by several rooms on her way down the hall. One had a grand piano with a massive candelabra atop it. Others were lined with ornate bookcases and display shelves. Still others were filled with all sorts of furniture.

But something wasn't quite right. While the room she started out in was bright, clean, and elaborately decorated, these other rooms seemed to have fallen into disrepair. The piano didn't appear to have any keys. The bookcases were empty, except for cobwebs. And all of the furniture was covered with dusty white sheets. The walls were bare and soiled in some places, covered with patches of stained, peeling wallpaper in others.

Selina took another step and found herself at the end of the hall, in the doorway to the room from which she had seen light coming. She heard a voice—more of a sound than an actual word—and stepped inside. In the far corner of the room was a small table with a Tiffany lamp radiating light through colored glass.

Beside the table was a wooden chair. Anya was tied to it, her wrists bound to the arms of the chair with rope, a ball-gag strapped across her face.

The door slammed shut behind Selina. Before she was able to turn around, something hit the back of her head, and the room went from dim to dark.

Selina woke up in a reclined position, but was unable to move with complete freedom. It was as if she was tangled up in something. As her eyes adjusted to the dim light from the lamp in the corner, she realized she was suspended a few feet above the floor, in a love swing hanging from the ceiling. Her wrists and ankles were tied into the web of fabric straps that formed a sort of sexual hammock. The type of thing some people—non-industry people—seemed to think was "kinky".

A rag had been stuffed into her mouth, deep enough she couldn't spit it out. She focused on breathing through her nose. Porn 101.

She heard a whimper. It was Anya, still tied to her chair. Selina must not have been out for too long. Anya's cheeks were streaked black and gray with the sort of lines that can only be formed by mascara blurred by tears.

Anya made another sound. She was trying to say something, but the ball-gag in her mouth made it nearly impossible. Selina figured out the puzzle quickly enough, though. It wasn't difficult. Anya was saying "I'm sorry. I'm so, so sorry."

Even in the dim light, Selina could tell the poor shape the room was in. It seemed as if most of the house's interior had been neglected for some time. The exterior was gorgeous, and the foyer and the room at the front of the house were beautifully kept, but everything else she had seen was far worse. It was like some extreme form of real estate bait and switch.

The floor creaked. Across the room, she saw a silhouette— what appeared to be a man in an overcoat. He also seemed to be wearing a large fedora.

"Hello, Miss Southgate," he said in a low voice.

11

"Wow, this place is amazing," Jesse said, truly impressed.

"Thanks," said Gagger. "My ex was an interior designer. I picked up a few tricks here and there."

Jesse was mesmerized by the lava lamp wall that had been installed instead of windows at the far end of the living room. It was essentially an aquarium for brightly colored molten wax.

Gagger returned from the kitchen.

"Dinner's almost ready," he said. "You like hot dogs, right?"

"Huh . . . what?" she said, pulling her attention away from the colorful, dancing blobs. For a second, she envisioned eating a hot dog slathered with ketchup and mustard and relish, and wondered why she had bothered getting dressed up the way she did. Spilling something on her dress would mean a hefty dry cleaning bill.

"I'm kidding," Gagger said with a chuckle. "Here. While you

wait." Gagger handed her a glass of Merlot. Jesse laughed, both at his joke and her own fixation on the lava, and thanked him, taking one of the two glasses in his hands. They tipped them toward each other, but didn't clink them together.

"Mmm," Gagger said after a sip. "I do love a good glass of wine."

Jesse felt a flutter inside. Not only was Gagger a gorgeous man, but he was also in the industry, meaning he understood her lifestyle. And on top of that, he was cultured. His home could be a magazine feature, and he apparently knew what he was doing in the kitchen.

She flashed forward to a future in which the two of them worked together during the day (he would of course be among the first men she'd offer a Jinx Pix contract to) and attended lavish parties at night, then returned to any one of their immaculately designed homes around the world. Of course they would travel. Maybe someday they would even have kids they could spoil on a daily basis.

"In fact, I love a good glass of wine almost as much as I love a good cock!" Gagger said. "Right, honey?"

Jesse didn't respond, still lost in her vision.

"Well, I need to get back in there, and make sure nothing burns. Keep looking around. Everything should be ready in a few."

Jesse blinked her eyes a few times to bring her mind back to the present. She shifted her focus to a series of shelves lining one wall. All of Gagger's movies were there on display. *Bear-ly Legal.*

Bear Conditioning. The Bear Apparent. Bare-Back Bear Back to the Future. The Bare 'n' Stained Bears. All seventeen installments of *Cummy Bears.* Even what appeared to be an adult parody of Disney's 1979 sci-fi adventure *The Black Hole.*

He had a few non-porn titles too, but they were all foreign films Jesse had never heard of. She scrunched her lips and stepped away from the movie shelves.

"You're sure you don't mind me looking around?" she asked. "Looks like you've got a lot of great stuff here, but I don't want to be nosy."

"Not at all. Collections are meant to be displayed, right? Explore. And ask any questions you like. Almost everything has a story."

Jesse moved into the next room. One wall was dotted with masks—everything from African tribal pieces to antique Japanese Kabuki props to vintage plastic Halloween masks for kids.

The rest of the room was filled with glass display cases and curio cabinets, the first of which contained rows and rows of gold and silver medallions.

"Flip the switch on the wall and the cases will light up," Gagger said from the kitchen.

She did this and heard harp music in her head as the room came alive with magic. She set her wine glass down on the floor and moved to the next case, where she found dozens of figurines, seemingly from various parts of the world. Some were clearly made from stone, others carved from wood or sculpted with clay.

In the next case she found matchbooks imprinted with a wide

variety of colors and logos in numerous languages. There were vials of ash with labels like "Mount Vesuvius", "Mount St. Helens", and "Mauna Loa".

"I had no idea you were such a collector," she called out. "I didn't realize I was coming to dinner at the freakin' Gagger Museum."

Jesse moved to the next display case and touched the surface of the glass with the tips of her fingers. Instantly, the lights inside all the cases in the room turned red, and an alarm sounded. It was far from ear-piercing, but still loud enough to let her know she had done something wrong. Jesse froze.

"Sorry! Sorry!" she said over the beeping, as Gagger bounded into the room. He punched a series of numbers into a keypad on the wall and everything stopped.

"No, I'm sorry," he said. "I should've turned that off."

"Heh . . . yeah, gave me a little scare," Jesse said with a deep exhale.

Gagger stepped over and gave her a one-arm side-hug. "Sorry, honey," he said, and kissed her temple.

"So, what's all this about?" she asked, gesturing toward the case she had just touched.

"Oh, those were my dad's," Gagger said. He opened the case so Jesse could get a better look inside. It was a shallow cabinet with a series of pins protruding from the back panel, to hold its contents. Inside, hanging salon-style, however they would fit, was a collection of axes and hatchets of all sizes. Some were clearly antiques, but others were somewhat newer. Most had handles of wood, beautifully stained. A few even had individual finger grooves carved into the handles.

"My dad was a lumberjack," Gagger said. "That's probably where I got my love of 'wood'." He laughed. "So, these were his tools. He made most of the handles himself, actually, from trees he cut down."

"Wow," Jesse said, never expecting that the evening would take a turn like this. Or that she would find a collection of axes the least bit interesting.

"He worked for years in the Pacific Northwest. Even when everyone else was using chainsaws, he stuck with what he knew, and the power of his own body swinging an axe. Probably chopped his way to an early grave that way, of course. But that's life, I suppose."

Gagger pulled one of the tools from the display and held it in his hands, feeling the weight of it.

"Anyway, this is what he left me when he died. My brothers got the house and his truck and everything else. But this was really all I wanted."

"Wow," Jesse said again. "I never would have guessed." Gagger handed her the axe he was holding so she could feel it in her own hands. She caught herself instinctively running one hand gently back and forth along the handle. After a moment, she handed the tool back to Gagger. "Beautiful," she said.

"Well," he said, replacing the axe and closing up the case, "you ready to eat?"

1 2

The nylon fabric straps holding Selina hostage creaked as she tried to free herself. The man in the overcoat standing before her didn't seem concerned. She wasn't going anywhere unless he decided to let her. She dangled from the ceiling, a sex toy having been converted into a prison. She felt like a fly caught in a spiderweb. She was scared. And the ever-so-slight circular motion of the swing was starting to turn her stomach.

Anya was still sobbing, still mumbling her apologies through the ball-gag.

"As I said, Miss Southgate . . . or should I say, Miss Gonzalez . . ." The man paused a moment to make sure Selina realized he knew her real name. "You and your friends have been walking down a very dangerous path. It's a shame you've made certain choices in your lives. Unfortunately they've led you to this moment."

Selina suddenly remembered Foxy's story about her creepy shoot in an empty house. The one she had dashed away from rather easily, but which had still left her quite shaken. *Was this the same guy? Was this the guy who had been murdering porn stars?*

She imagined someone slapping her across the face. After all, could this be anyone else? Of course it was him. She struggled again with her bonds.

"I've got something for you, Miss Gonzalez," the man said.

Selina couldn't see his face, but couldn't determine if that was due to the low light in the room, or because he was wearing some sort of mask. There was a small glint of light over his eyes, but the rest of his face was in shadow. Perhaps he was wearing some sort of black stocking to hide his identity.

He stepped toward the doorway. Beside it, in the corner, there seemed to be a small table with something on it. The love swing turned a bit, and for the moment, Selina couldn't see what the man was doing.

A second later, he turned around, holding what appeared to be a very large cock and balls. An enormous dildo, at least a foot long—maybe more—and far thicker than anything she had seen in real life. It was clear, she could tell, even in the low light. She saw a small plume of mist rise off it. *Was it made of ice?*

"No doubt this looks familiar to you, dear," the man said, holding the object in his black leather gloves. "But I doubt you've seen one quite like this. You've never seen one so crystal clear, so clean. *So pure.* Have you?"

Selina responded with a scream, but it was dampened by the

rag in her mouth.

Anya whimpered too and shook her arms against the ropes holding her to her chair. She rocked back and forth, bumping the table next to her. A small piece of colored glass fell from the lamp to the table, allowing a tiny bit more light out to shine across the room.

"Oh, you hush over there, Miss Lapinski," the man said, using Anya's real name while angrily pointing a gloved finger in her direction. He nearly dropped the dildo in the process, but brought his hand back just in time. "I'll get back to you soon enough."

He returned his attention to Selina.

"I'm going to purify you with this," the man said. As he stepped toward her, she saw past him, and was able to make out the object on the table, where he had gotten the ice dildo. It was a cooler, made of blue and white plastic. It had the words "Lunch Box" on the side, crossed out and replaced with "Munch Box", written by hand in black marker.

"This here? This is made from holy water," Peter said. "I assume this is the only form you'll take it in, *you filthy cunt!"*

Peter? she thought. She screamed inside her own head. *Peter the PA?* He closed in on her.

Selina shook violently with everything she had, but she remained restrained, and the swing turned only slightly. A puff of plaster dust drifted down from above.

Peter removed the rag from Selina's mouth. She screamed as loud as she could, but her voice was stifled immediately by the tip of the dildo pressing past her lips, colliding with her front teeth, then sliding across her tongue, and deep into her mouth. It was cold, of course, and the hot breath from her nostrils caused condensation to rise from it, clouding her already limited vision in the dimly lit room. The tears that had begun to form in her eyes didn't help either.

Peter pushed the tube of ice deeper into Selina's mouth, and she felt it press into the top of her throat. She closed her eyes hard and tried to focus on breathing through her nose. Then Peter squeezed her nostrils shut.

"Now, now," he said. "Let's not adulterate the purity of this moment. Just accept what I'm feeding you. Let it soothe you. Let it cool you. It's the only way to not end up burning for all eternity."

Selina tried to pull in a breath, but couldn't. She wriggled, fighting against the restraints, but she was tied up firmly, and Peter's grip was strong. This was going to be it. This was how her story would come to an end. In a tangle of fabric straps, at the hands of a maniac. Worst of all, it was someone she knew. She opened her eyes and looked directly into his. They burned with fury.

The light in the room changed suddenly. Anya popped up from the chair, having cut her ropes with the fallen shard of glass from the lamp beside her. She took three steps and swung the rest of the Tiffany lamp down on Peter's head. Bits of colored glass went everywhere.

The momentum of her act brought Anya down on top of Peter, and Peter down onto Selina. The ceiling instantly gave out where the love swing dangled, and they all crashed to the floor as bits of plaster cascaded down on top of them. Peter landed head-first. He was out. Selina was dazed, but conscious. She was suddenly able to breathe through her nose again.

Anya stood back up and felt for Selina's head in the darkness. She extracted the dildo from Selina's mouth, then tossed it across the room. They heard it hit the wall and break into several pieces, which then fell to the floor and scattered across the uneven planks of wood. Selina gasped, pulling in as much air as she could, then burped.

Anya laughed through the ball-gag, still strapped to her face, and made her way to the door. She opened it, allowing a small amount of light from the front room of the house to leak down the hall and in. It was still very dim, but they could see something, at least.

Anya returned to Selina, grabbing a larger piece of broken glass from the now-shattered lamp, and used it to saw away at the straps binding one of Selina's wrists. Once that arm was free, she handed the glass to Selina, and they both worked to cut away the rest of her bindings. A moment later, Selina wriggled herself out of the love swing's netting.

Anya undid the buckles on her head and tossed the gag aside too. She wiped her lips.

"I'm so sorry," she said, frantic. "He threatened to kill me if I didn't lure someone else in. He was hiding in the hall when I let you into the house. He said he had a gun on me."

Selina nodded.

"Let's get the fuck out of here," she said quietly, and started for the door.

Anya was right behind her, but stopped for a second to deliver a kick to Peter's ribs. "Asshole," she said, then stepped over him, to follow Selina out.

But Peter had regained consciousness. He grabbed Anya's ankle in mid-stride, and she fell ninety degrees, her nose crunching as it smashed directly into the floor. Peter pushed himself up to his knees. Plaster dust rained down from the crooked brim of his hat. His overcoat had more of it caked in the folds.

Selina's eyes widened as she turned back, grabbing the sides of the doorframe. She already knew they didn't have much time to escape the house, but thought they'd at least make it outside before Peter woke up.

Anya tried to stand, but Peter shoved a hand into the middle of her back and stood up himself instead.

Selina looked around for a weapon, fighting the urge to bolt, but there wasn't much to be seen.

Anya looked up, blood streaming from her nose, and screamed "Go!" just before Peter stomped a boot down on the back of her neck with a wet pop.

Selina grabbed the cooler off the table by the door and threw it with both hands. Her aim was good. It crashed into Peter's head, only partially blocked by his hands, and he fell backward.

Selina ran. She ran down the dark hall, past the neglected rooms, then through the nicely decorated room at the front of the house. She undid the lock on the front door and ran out. She had been inside for hours. It was getting dark now.

She reached the side of her car and realized her bag was still inside the house. She didn't have her keys. Panic ratcheted up a notch with this realization. She had no choice but to keep running.

Fifteen Years Earlier

Peter Pedersen, not yet a teenager, sat on the edge of the guest room bed, the covers in disarray, his back to the bedroom door. He sat there, in front of the TV, one eye over his shoulder, one hand tugging away at himself for the very first time. He struggled to keep quiet while enjoying these new sensations, knowing his parents were just downstairs, his mother stirring something in a pot on the stove.

His family still owned a VCR and a box full of video cassettes, which Peter's father had recently rediscovered while cleaning out the garage. Since then, Peter had been going through the tapes, many of which were unmarked, to see what sort of treasures they contained.

And oh, what treasures he had found. Many of the tapes had

three movies apiece, all recorded from TV in the 1980s. Horror movies, action movies, and the occasional raunchy comedy, many recorded off the movie-centric pay channels, although a handful had been taped elsewhere and came complete with vintage commercials. Some of the movies were rarities, having never been released on any form of home video since the days of VHS. One tape in particular, though, was the Holy Grail for Peter.

His father clearly hadn't bothered to pre-screen any of the tapes before letting his son have at them. He probably remembered the action movies and some monster madness, but he must not have realized he handed his son a copy of *Charles Dick-In's A Tale of Two Titties*, a porn flick. This was a store-bought pre-recorded tape, although the label had at some point been removed.

Of course, Peter knew what sex was, at least in some abstract way. His father had given him a vague talk about the birds and the bees at some point, but he had learned more from some of the kids at school. And he had read a fairly lurid description of the female body in a book, or magazine, or something, somewhere.

But this tape was something else. It was full-on, hardcore nudity and penetration. Peter had never seen this before. It was a little scary, but exciting.

Before he knew it, his hand was reaching down the front of his shorts. He rubbed himself as a woman on the screen with a blue and white headband bounced up and down on some thickly mustached man's lap.

Seeing the woman's large, natural breasts bounce, keeping

time in jiggly orbits, made Peter more and more excited, made him stroke himself faster and faster, until, suddenly, he found himself laughing out loud, as waves of pleasure rolled through him for the first time. Peter shot several arcs of hot semen into the air, not quite knowing what was happening. Their paths ended abruptly on the bottom edge of the TV screen, blurring spots of the moving image.

It was at precisely that moment Peter's mother had decided to enter the room, to let him know dinner was ready.

"Peter, honey," she said, before screaming something more bloodcurdlingly appropriate for a monster movie on one of the other tapes. From there, she uttered a series of *"What?!"s* and *"What are you doing?!"s.*

Peter thought she was upset she had caught him watching a dirty movie, caught him masturbating. She was more upset she had caught him masturbating to one of *her* old movies, something she had done prior to married life, prior to starting a family.

She screamed again, consumed with an irrational fury, and stormed toward her son. Peter, startled, lost his balance from the edge of the mattress, his legs tangled in his shorts and the bedsheets, and fell to the floor, bumping his head on the edge of the TV stand, as he landed in a small puddle of his own semen.

"What are you doing?! Why are you watching me?!" his mother screamed, her eyes growing wide and wild. "Why are you watching *meeeeeeeee?!*"

Peter scrambled on the floor, struggling to hide his waning

erection and pull up his pants. *What was she talking about?* The woman on the screen was some actress from the '80s.

Peter's mother ran to the TV and frantically punched the Eject button on the VCR a dozen or more times, until the TV screen flipped to static and the once state-of-the-art but now-obsolete machine spat out the tape. She yanked it from the slot and held it up beside her face, screaming, manic. She bared her teeth and continued yelling.

"Whyyyyyy?! Why would you jerk off to your mother?! You sick child! You pervert! Why? Why are you watching me?!"

Peter began screaming too, all fear and embarrassment. Tears began streaming down his face.

"ImsorryImsorryImsorryImsorry . . ."

His mother, tape in hand, swung her arm back, screaming *"YOU SICK FUCK! Don't you ever fucking— Why are you watching . . . meeeeeeeeee?!"* Then she swung her arm forward with great force and slammed the tape into the screen of the television. The cassette shattered instantly and black plastic splinters shot in all directions. One of them hit Peter's mother in the eye. Another landed on the tip of his penis. Magnetic tape unspooled from what was left of the tape in his mother's hand, and zig-zagged across Peter's legs.

Mother and son shrieked in unison, and something happened inside Peter's brain.

14

"And the police were no help?" Jesse asked. She handed a pair of coffee mugs to Selina and Foxy. "Those bastards. Unbelievable. Riley and I got the brush-off too, when we went in asking about Dina. But that was weeks ago. Bodies have been piling up."

"No. Pinche idiota," said Selina, almost unwilling to believe it herself. "I walk in there bloody and bruised, nearly killed by some fucking pendejo, and this Knowles asshole starts asking me if I'm even a US citizen. Then he asks what kind of drugs I take on a regular basis."

"Fucking bullshit," said Foxy, sipping her coffee. "That's why I didn't even bother going to the cops when I had my run-in. I didn't feel like dealing with the *'What were you doing in that neighborhood?'* bullshit."

"And it only got worse when I started telling him about the fucking ice dildo. Can you believe that shit? I mean, *an ice dildo?*

An ice dildo made from *holy water*? What the fuck is that?"

"A weapon that leaves no trace of itself," said Foxy, taking another sip, her other arm folded across her stomach as if she was giving herself a hug. "A weapon made of ice will melt away." She paused a moment. "I can't believe this. And what are the odds we both got away from the same lunatic?"

"I even told this cop who he was," Selina continued. "I told him where the house was. I told him about Anya. About your experience. Everything. And he's like, 'You know, you really shouldn't be walking around in such short shorts . . .'"

"I can't believe it's Peter the PA!" interrupted Jesse. *"Peter the fucking PA! He was always so nice. I thought he just liked to watch! Holy shit!"*

"Literally," said Selina. "He's like some underground secret agent for Jesus or something."

"Or he's just insane," said Foxy. "Either way, we need to do something about this, since nobody else seems to care too much about a bunch of dead porn stars. Or even a few nearly-killed porn stars."

"So what do we do? Start packing heat?" Selina asked. "Where do we even buy a gun?"

"Well, they're easy enough to get," Foxy said. "But I'm not a big fan. The thing's more likely to go off in my purse than I am to fish it out in time if someone's trying to shove something down my throat."

"Yeah, guns terrify me," said Jesse. "My uncle took me hunting one time when I was a kid. No thanks."

"Well we've got to do something," said Selina.

"Of course! But are we gonna start showing up to shoots ready to shoot?" said Jesse. "I mean, that's gonna make some people pretty uncomfortable. And there's only so many places to hide a gun when you're lying naked across a countertop anyway."

"If the police aren't going to help, we need to take care of this ourselves, and we can't wait around," said Selina.

"I think we need to set a trap," said Foxy. "He probably realizes you know who he is, right? He's probably going to be coming back for you, to shut you up once and for all."

"Shit. And I left my bag in that house," said Selina, shivering. "*He's got my address.*"

"Okay. So we need to act fast," said Foxy. "Like now."

"Hang on a second," said Jesse. "If you're both serious about this, I have an idea. *And I just might know someone who can hook us up.*"

1 5

Selina stayed at Jesse's place that night. The company, not to mention the security system, made Selina feel safe. Foxy stayed over too, and she and Jesse offset the hours of their sleep so one of them was awake at any given point all night, just in case.

The next night, however, Selina was back at home. She went about her business, responding to some emails from fans, and looking at the design comps for her website, which she was hoping to relaunch soon. She cooked a small dinner and ate it on the couch, where she settled in for an evening of TV. She said something to herself about her DVR being full. She needed to either binge-watch something or start deleting.

She was nervous, sitting there, trying to act natural, knowing Peter was standing right outside, spying at her through the window of her first floor apartment in the house. But she knew she was a better actor than most of the girls in the industry, and she kept the ruse going.

Peter began breathing heavy as he watched Selina through the glass. He tried not to get too close, so his breath wouldn't fog up the windowpane. The blinds were down, but not completely closed, so he was able to see everything through the cracks between the strips of vinyl.

He watched as Selina started playing the new season of *Mouse Houses* and burrowed herself into the couch cushions. After a few minutes, she reached over and clicked off the lamp on the end table. The TV offered the only illumination in the room, something she felt might lure Peter in.

Peter decided the time was right. He stepped out of the bushes by the window and circled around to the other side of the house. He was pleasantly surprised at how poorly lit the exterior of the building was. Dressed in his usual black overcoat, he went undetected by neighbors.

Selina was determined to stay on guard, despite the fact she was beginning to get lost in the first episode of *Mouse Houses*. The host was a very charming middle-aged man with an Australian accent who built tiny houses for disadvantaged little people, free of charge. The concept behind the show was wonderful, she thought, except for the title, which was rather offensive, not to mention an extremely odd choice on the part of the producer. Not that she hadn't seen her share of unusual titles.

She perked up when she heard a sound come from the direction of her bedroom. *Had Peter found a way in already? Or was it just the house settling?* Her upstairs neighbors were out of town on vacation, so it couldn't have been them.

Selina sat up, moving her feet from the end of the couch to the floor.

"Hello?" she asked aloud, wondering if she would receive a response.

She leaned forward, but couldn't stand up. Peter, already in the room, pulled her back with a hand across her jaw.

She tried to scream through the gloved hand, but the sound was muffled. She tried to lean forward again, but Peter was too strong. With just one hand, he was able to keep Selina pinned to the couch. From the corner of her eye, she could see his other hand, holding one of his signature ice dildos. She didn't get a very close look, but this one seemed even bigger than the last. Maybe it was just the blue light of the TV distorting her perspective.

Selina wriggled and bucked, trying to at least turn her body around, if she wasn't able to get up completely. She needed to be facing him.

"Hey asshole!" Foxy said, emerging from the bedroom. Jesse echoed the line as she popped up from behind the kitchen island, flicking the light switch on the wall.

Peter was surprised, enough that his grip loosened slightly, and Selina was able to free herself. She spun around and stood up, taking a step back from Peter. Her arm shot between the couch cushions and retrieved her secret weapon, an axe.

Jesse stepped out from behind the kitchen counter and revealed herself to be holding an axe as well. Foxy had a third hidden behind one leg. The three women brandished their weapons like samurai. Peter raised his frozen weapon to hold it up the same way.

The moment lasted only a second, as Peter pump-faked toward Selina, and she reacted with a wild swing, whiffing. She had envisioned a perfect connection, but the reality was, this was the first time she'd swung an axe, and the weight at the end of it threw her off balance.

Selina fell back down onto the couch, as her weapon slipped from her fingers to the floor. Peter jumped on top of her immediately and pinned her down with a heavy foot in the middle of her back.

Foxy and Jesse both charged, but hesitated, each thinking the other would swing first. Peter took advantage of the moment, swinging the ice dildo one direction into Jesse's ribs, then quickly back the other way, slamming into Foxy's shoulder. Jesse doubled over in pain, while Foxy was knocked off balance sideways.

Peter, still holding Selina down with one foot, turned his body back toward Jesse, expecting her to offer the next attack. But it was Foxy who righted herself first and unleashed everything she had through the weapon in her hands. She connected with the base of Peter's skull, but hit him with the blunt, butt end of the axe instead of the blade. It was a heavy shot, and knocked him to the floor, groaning as he fell face-first into the carpet.

Selina, no longer restrained, popped up quickly, axe in hand.

"Thanks," she said, taking a deep breath.

"You okay over there?" Foxy asked.

Jesse tried to stand straight, but was having difficulty. She nodded and raised a hand in affirmation, taking a deep breath of her own.

"Maybe the cops'll believe us now," Foxy said, turning back to Selina. "You want to call them?"

Selina nodded, and stepped across the room to get her phone.

Foxy took a look at the unconscious body of their attacker on the floor in front of the couch, then turned toward Jesse, who was hugging her belly.

"You sure you're okay, girl?" Foxy said. "Try to stand up straight, and just focus on deep breaths for a minute. Here, breathe with me."

Then Foxy got hit with a column of ice. Peter had once again regained consciousness quickly, and with one swing, shattered his weapon over the porn star's head. She certainly felt it, but her adrenaline was already pumping, so it wasn't enough to take her out.

All three women pounced. They came at Peter from three different directions and started swinging, this time without any hesitation. The killer fell into the couch, and the trio of porn stars settled into a rhythm with their axes. *Thunk-thunk-thunk, thunk-thunk-thunk.* They laughed as they delivered each blow, their violent climax reaching full tilt. Blood spurted into the air and across their hands and faces. A minute later, Peter had been hacked to pieces.

Finally their rhythm slowed, and they stopped. There was no more point. Peter was ground meat in a shredded black overcoat. They stood there, and looked down at the bloody pile of flesh and guts, and let the axes fall to the carpet, *thunk-thunk-thunk.*

"We got him," Jesse said.

"Fucking bastard," Foxy said.

"Mierda," Selina said. "I'm gonna need a new couch."

1 6

Ivana Zukyov and Crystal Balls met for the first time, years ago, about an hour before they were supposed to have sex. That's how things were in this industry. Sex was the job. You had to think of it in a different way than most people did. There was nothing romantic about it. There was nothing serious about it. There was nothing to get hung up about. It was just the job.

That didn't mean you couldn't have fun at work, of course. But it wasn't necessarily the goal. You just had to convince other people you were enjoying it.

Ivana and Crystal did have fun with it, though. They were about to shoot their twenty-seventh (or was it twenty-eighth?) scene together, if the crew ever showed up.

"Who set this one up? Marty?" Crystal asked.

"I think so," said Ivana. "I just go where the emails tell me to go." She smiled.

Ivana had come to America with plans to be a model. At first, she had hustled her way into a few photo shoots. Those eventually led to some nude photo shoots. From there, it didn't take long for her to find her way into dancing at gentlemen's clubs. And she discovered she found that far more exciting, taking off her clothes for complete strangers while working a pole on stage. She loved it.

Of course, that soon led to porn, and it was as if Ivana had finally found her calling. She didn't care what other people thought of her. She didn't care that people back home thought she had failed in her quest to become a model. She had come to this country to find herself, really, and find herself she did. Only, along the way, she found what she truly wanted to be.

Ivana loved the ability to be free. She loved she could do what she wanted with her body, and—at least among her small circle of friends and colleagues—not be judged for it. She loved experiencing new sensations and trying new things.

She enjoyed the sex she had with her friend Crystal. She enjoyed it back when Crystal Balls was known as Chris Tickle, and she enjoyed it now that Crystal had begun her transition. Life was an adventure, and Ivana was happy to be living.

Ivana did not expect to go use the bathroom, then return to find her friend Crystal tied up with a rag in her mouth. And whomever she expected to see at this shoot, it certainly wasn't a man dressed in a black overcoat and fedora.

1 7

"It is with a heavy heart that I call you here tonight, my friends." The man speaking stood at the pulpit of a small abandoned church. The building itself had fallen into disrepair over the years, left to rot in a corner of the city that few frequented, despite the fact that available real estate was at an all-time low.

The moon above was full and shone into the church through a hole in the building's roof.

The man wore a black overcoat, black gloves, a black stocking over his face, and a black fedora on his head.

A crowd of several dozen were assembled before him, standing where pews were once anchored. They were all dressed the same way, their overcoats, hats, and obscured faces like some sort of uniform or sacred attire.

"As you were all well aware upon joining The Order of Purity, our cause is a righteous one, but the path is a dangerous one.

"I'm sorry to inform you all that Brother Peter has fallen at the hands of those we have been trying to eradicate from our otherwise respectable society."

A wave of sadness enveloped the crowd. Several people shook their heads in disbelief.

"These wasted souls are, indeed, more detrimental to our community than we had feared," the man continued. "It seems at least one of these disgusting agents of sin has now taken up arms of her own, in an effort to defend her filthy way of life, vile as it may be.

"So I ask you to ramp up your efforts! I realize each of us has our own unique reasons for doing what we are doing. But our goal is a common one. We must extract these filthy whores from our society and send them on their way to oblivion!"

In the distance, thunder rumbled, and a dark cloud passed in front of the moon.

"In seven days, as many of you already know, much of the so-called 'adult industry' will be assembled for a world-record attempt at orgiastic depravity. A filthy, disgusting display of the most heinous sexual acts imaginable. A tapestry of flesh and fluids.

"This is our chance. This is an opportunity. Those of us who have already infiltrated the industry will lead the charge, while the rest of us will be waiting in the wings. In seven days, we shall remove the dirt from our community in one fell swoop.

"Between now and then, Brothers and Sisters, freeze your instruments. And remember we use frozen water as a symbol of purity. We must use it to freeze the evil inside them. We must freeze the vile intent in their hearts before the fires of Hell overtake us all!"

Rain began to fall suddenly, a few drops at first, then a downpour. Water streamed into the church through the massive hole in the roof as well as a hundred cracks and splits throughout the aged structure.

"So go, Brothers and Sisters! Go now!" the man shouted over the storm. "Freeze your instruments, and prepare, for our day comes soon!"

1 8

"I just wish there had been some sort of reward money," said Jesse, returning to H.R. Gagger's living room from the kitchen, her hands clasped around three glasses of water.

"There's no reward money when no one cares," Selina replied, carefully taking the foremost beverage from Jesse's hands. "The police thought we were pranking them when we said someone needed to come pick up all the body parts on my couch."

"Good thing you had those heavy-duty trash bags," Jesse said. "This shit is ridiculous." She handed a glass to Foxy, and another to Gagger, then returned to the kitchen for her own.

"You girls are hardcore," Gagger said.

"Maybe we can start a porn star militia or something," said Foxy. "People can hire us to take out the bad guys *and* look sexy doing it. There's gotta be some money in that." Foxy laughed, barely able to keep a straight face through the end of her thought.

Jesse laughed too. But it wasn't a horrible idea. At the very least, it was a feature concept for Jinx Pix.

"Anyway, thanks again, Gagger," she said, returning to the living room once again. "And sorry it took a few days to get these back to you. We've been laying low, obviously."

"Happy to help. I just hope I can get the blood stains out of the handles," Gagger said, examining one of the axes he had leant out. The other two were still inside the canvas tote bag Jesse had used to transport them. He picked at a spot of dried blood with a fingernail. "I'm not sure that was a problem my dad ever had in his line of work."

Even days later, Selina was still shaken, but happy the ordeal was over. "I can't believe I have to go furniture shopping. Mierda."

"Well, it's a good thing we've got *The Big Bang* tomorrow!" Jesse pointed out. "Money, honey!"

"You seem a little upbeat for someone who recently hacked a maniac into pieces with an axe." Foxy sipped her water.

"Sorry," Jesse said. "Violence makes me horny."

"You're crazy, girl," said Foxy. "I can't believe I'm going to let you be my boss someday."

Jesse smiled, bumping her eyebrows up and down.

The doorbell rang, and Gagger popped up to answer it.

"There's lunch, ladies," he said. "Jesse, can you grab some plates? I'll be right back with the food."

"Well, that 'someday' should be coming along pretty soon,"

said Jesse, responding to Foxy's remark. "I was actually just looking over my business plan again last night, and I think I can make things work after just a few more—"

Jesse was interrupted by a loud, wall-shaking thump, then the sound of glass breaking. The three women froze and looked at each other with concern.

"Gagger?" Selina called out. "Everything okay?"

Another slam shook the house, and they heard what sounded like a man's voice angrily saying "Take it, take it".

The women dashed toward the front door, and found Gagger on his knees, his head tilted back, with an enormous dildo made of ice jammed down his throat. A large man dressed in black stood before him, one hand grasping Gagger's hair, and the other holding the massive shaft of ice in place, choking him. He wore an overcoat, leather gloves, a stocking over his face, and a large fedora, just like Peter had.

The man hadn't expected three more people to be there, however. Startled, he stood where he was for a second, then let go of Gagger and the dildo, and ran off.

Gagger fell the rest of the way to the floor and lay on his side, his head still pushed back by the thing in his throat.

Foxy ran out the door after the attacker, and gave chase for half a block, screaming the whole way. But the assailant was fast, and disappeared quickly around a corner.

Jesse and Selina leapt toward Gagger as he tipped over from his side onto his belly. Jesse grabbed his shoulder and tried to roll him back so they could remove the ice from his throat and save him.

But Gagger stirred, and pushed his way up to his knees himself, then leaned back and deftly removed the dildo from his throat like a professional sword swallower at the end of his act. He wiped his lips with the back of his arm and took a moment to catch his breath.

"I'm fine," he said, smacking his lips. "That bastard didn't know who he was dealing with."

"What do we do? *What the fuck do we do?!*" Selina was frantic, pacing back and forth across the room. "I thought this was all over!"

The dildo was in Gagger's bathroom, slowly melting in the tub, because it was too large for the sink.

"I know," said Foxy. "Me too. We need to stay calm."

"Stay calm? *Stay calm?!*" said Jesse. Her face was nearly as red as her hair. "We just killed this fucker a few days ago, *and now he shows up at the front door!*"

"I mean we need to focus," Foxy said. "Look, that wasn't Peter. Peter's dead. We made sure of that."

"Yeah, that guy was a lot bigger than Peter anyway," said Selina. Her hands were shaking, so she dug them into her pockets.

"Strong as hell too," said Gagger, rubbing the back of his neck.

"So . . . what? This guy's a copycat?" Jesse said.

"How could there be a copycat? None of this stuff was publicized. The cops didn't even believe it was happening," said Selina.

"Good point. What then?" asked Jesse.

"Well, it's obvious there's more than one," Foxy said. "But are there more than two?"

"Looks like they've got uniforms. I'd be willing to bet there are at least a few more," said Gagger.

"Oh great. So we're just going to have to worry about this for the rest of our lives, huh?" Jesse said.

"I'm not planning on it," said Foxy.

1 9

"You feeling alright today?" asked Mel. She was applying make-up to an endless line of women in lightweight robes down the hall from the soundstage. Not that she was making any extra money for it. She got paid by the shoot, not by how many cheeks she made rosy.

"Yeah, I'm fine," said Jesse, lying.

"You just seem a little nervous today, that's all," Mel continued. "I thought maybe you finally got sick of doing this crap." Mel was her typical grumpy self.

"I'm good, Mel. Thanks," Jesse said. "Hey, I've got this bruise on my side, here. Maybe you could cover it up with the airbrush? Try not to cover up my tats, though."

Mel didn't respond, but gave Jesse a look. She reached for her airbrush.

"You know, I realize this isn't your thing, Mel," Jesse said. "I realize maybe you wouldn't feel comfortable doing this kind of stuff on camera. But some of us really do enjoy it. And we don't like to be preached to right before we go on camera."

"You still look nervous," Mel said. "But I can't cover that up."

"I'm not sure why you keep coming back," Jesse said. She stood up and pulled her robe closed.

"Okay, Miss Jinx, if you're ready, I'll show you to your spot," said Lucy, one of the Production Assistants for the shoot. Jesse was led down the hall to the soundstage. Arrows made from glow-in-the-dark tape showed the way, but it was Lucy's duty to make sure everyone was escorted.

This was by far the largest production Jesse had ever been a part of, and it seemed like the entire industry was here. *The Big Bang*. Every major production company had joined forces for the ultimate orgy. She didn't even know what the plot of the film was supposed to be—if there was one—only that every porn star she knew was supposed to be part of it. Even from a distance, she recognized Phoenix Firecrotch. She spotted Keiko Kink and Leia Onnerbach too. And Heidi Ho.

"Hey, babe," said Foxy. She was wearing a purple robe. Selina was standing beside her in a semi-transparent red robe, with a duffel bag hanging off her shoulder.

Lucy the PA continued walking, but Jesse stopped to talk with her friends. "Hey, uh . . ." she called ahead. "Buck said it's okay if we bring toys, right?" Lucy hadn't realized Jesse had stopped moving behind her.

Jesse reached into the bag on Selina's shoulder and revealed the end of a brown dildo to show her. "It's okay, right?"

Lucy the PA nodded, then said, "We need to get you all into position. Buck wants to start shooting in the next ten minutes."

"What about all the girls still in line for make-up?" Jesse asked.

"They'll be joining in soon enough. Buck wants to get started with some featured close-ups before everybody gets sweaty. He'll pull back for the wider shots later."

"I'm not sure how I feel about this," Selina said, as Lucy tied her wrists to a red cargo net. She had been tied up before, of course, but her most recent experience was in an abandoned house with a killer. "I didn't realize this was going to be a bondage thing."

"It's random," Lucy said. "Some people are getting tied up, some are getting DP'd, some are just licking slits the whole time. Someone will untie you at some point, and you'll be able to move around later."

"Can I trade for a DP instead?" Selina said.

"Sorry, hon. You're already locked in, and I've got a bunch of other folks I need to set up in the next couple minutes."

The set was simple. Beds, couches, and cushions had all been assembled side-by-side and front-to-back across a wide plot of the soundstage floor. Mattresses were stacked up to various heights, with the taller piles toward the back of the room, creating a sort of topographical island of fuck-space, all covered by a single gigantic, seemingly custom-sewn bright red sheet. The director, Buck Cadillac, was a big fan of the artist, Christo.

More like a drop cloth, Selina thought to herself, as she strained against the bindings on her wrists. She was already beginning to feel sore, and the sex hadn't even started yet.

She was at the back of the set, the cargo net suspended alongside the tallest stack of mattresses. The net was the same color red as everything else. She looked around and saw various cushions and pillows—some heart-shaped, others designed to look like cartoon penises and vaginas—all the same color, designed to blend into the background, so the focus was largely on the performers, as if that was something the director really needed to worry about.

Selina looked across the swath of red and spotted Foxy at one of the front corners of the set, bent over a wedge-shaped cushion, wiggling her ass back and forth to tease the guy standing behind her. Selina recognized his face and his cock—she had worked with him before—but couldn't remember his name. He stood there, stroking himself to a semi, his unit bulbous, but not yet ready to stand at attention.

Jesse was on the other side of the set from Foxy. She was seated on the edge of a two-mattress stack, scanning the room, clearly a bit nervous.

Selina shared the feeling. They all knew anything could happen at any moment. It wasn't a guarantee, of course, but with so many adult performers in one place at one time, the odds seemed high.

But it was also possible the recent killings were just a pair of unhinged people, one of whom had already been dealt with. There was a security guard at the entrance to the soundstage, and there were plenty of people around, on both sides of the cameras. It would probably be best to enjoy the day and give a good performance, but to certainly stay on guard.

Riley walked past where Jesse was sitting and waved.

"Oh, hey," Jesse said. "I didn't realize you were going to be here."

"I couldn't miss this," Riley said. "Good exposure, right? Everybody's gonna see this thing."

"Yeah, definitely. I just thought you were still visiting your parents."

"I got back this morning," Riley said. "Took the redeye."

"Looks like you got some new ink while you were gone too, huh?"

Riley instinctively rubbed her new tattoo, a brightly colored lotus on her shoulder.

"Yeah, I know this killer artist back home, and he always gives me a deal. You like?"

"Looks hot," said Jesse.

"Thanks," said Riley. "Hey, I better grab a good spot. Let's catch up later."

Jesse nodded, and Riley trekked across the landscape of flesh and cushions.

"Okay, everyone," Buck Cadillac announced, quieting the murmur of porn stars in the room. "I'm your director for the afternoon. If we haven't met personally, I'm sorry, but there's obviously quite a few of you here. It's going to be a fun day, so keep those smiles pretty.

"If you don't already have a partner, or a couple partners, turn to the person beside you and shake their hand, because you're about to fuck them. Guys, if your collars aren't starched yet, get a move on, or ask for some help. We're rolling in three minutes."

Selina adjusted her position on the net, getting slightly more comfortable, although there wasn't much she could do about the straps digging into her heels.

"Hey, doll," said Channing Totem. "Need a partner?"

Selina had seen Channing in action before, but they had never worked together. She thought he was cute, and felt a little flutter within, which helped to at least temporarily quell the pain in the small of her back.

"Sure." Selina bit her lower lip to suppress too big a smile. "Not that I have much choice at the moment," she said, wiggling her wrists.

"Well, I'll try not to take too much advantage," Channing said with a chuckle. "Say 'rhubarb' if I do something you don't like."

Selina nodded.

"Alright, we're rolling in thirty seconds," announced the director. "Anyone without a stiffy, get out of frame in a jiffy. There's a line of studs here on either side ready to tag in."

"Fancy meeting you here," Jesse said. Rod Almondjoy had

just climbed onto the set. He was standing beside her, and standing at full attention.

"Hey, Jesse," Rod said. "Wanna dance?"

Jesse reached for Rod's erection, and used it to guide him over to the stack of mattresses she had been sitting on just a few moments earlier. She sat him down, then climbed up and threw one leg over his shoulder, placing her vagina directly on his mouth. He was ready for her, and began massaging her clit softly with the tip of his tongue. Her eyes rolled back instantly, but she also told herself not to lose herself completely in the moment.

"We've got three roaming cameras in play right now," Buck continued. "Try to avoid eye contact with them. They'll be focusing on close-ups for a while, and more people will be filtering in as they come out of make-up. Eventually we'll pull back for some wider shots. Feel free to move around and change partners as often as you like. And we're rolling! Do what you do, and have fun doing it!"

The man behind Foxy had never been able to get it up, so a new guy had swapped in. He was rock hard and huge, and he pressed into Foxy slowly. She moaned, pressing her face into a cushion as he entered her. It took a minute for her to get used to his girth.

"Hey honey. What's your name?" she asked, eventually.

"Linc," he said. "Lincoln Logjam. Nice to meet you, Foxy. Big fan."

"You sure are," replied Foxy, before burying her face back into the cushion in front of her.

Before long, everyone in the room was moaning, the sounds of pleasure as thick in the air as the scent of sex. It wasn't just acting for the cameras. Everyone was truly happy to be a part of the big event.

Jesse had changed positions and partners several times over the course of the past half hour, and had legitimately orgasmed three times already. Once a guy popped, he left the set, at least temporarily, and another actor waiting in the wings climbed up onto the red island with his hard-on.

Jesse had never seen so many male actors before. In this business, there always seemed to be a small but reliable pool of guys who could fuck on camera and be any good at it. *Maybe they held some sort of contest for this movie,* she thought. *Maybe some of these guys weren't pros.*

She dismounted her current partner and moved to let him bend her over a short stack of cushions so he could take her from behind. She glanced across the set and saw Riley in a similar position. They made eye contact and Riley winked.

Foxy was also on the other side of the set, lying on her back, with a guy who went by the name Peckerpacker pumping away at her pelvis, while she tilted her head back to lap away at the snatch of a woman she had not yet exchanged names with.

Selina was still bound to her cargo net along the top edge of the red space. Amber Gold had climbed up beside her and somehow managed to make both of them cum without either falling.

Selina closed her eyes for a moment, enjoying the last moments of tingling before the sensation began to subside.

She whispered into Amber's ear, asking her to untie her. Her wrists were raw at this point, and she didn't like being confined, but she was also eager for a change of position.

Selina looked across the soundstage. She saw that Channing Totem had recharged and was now sixty-nining with a young goth starlet named Doomy Baby. She also spotted Heidi Ho grinding away on top of Roger Rammer, while she stroked Jeff Jammer's shaft. In the middle of it all, she spotted Rod Longshaft doing Kayla Cumbersnatch from behind. She had heard he was sick recently, and was glad to see he was feeling better.

She saw various members of the crew standing just past the edges of the red sex-scape—cameramen, lighting riggers, and boom operators, all watching the festivities intently. Gagger was there too. He wasn't taking part in the day's proceedings, but had come to offer support, and an extra pair of eyes in case something went wrong.

Along both sides of the soundstage were lines of nude men with erections, each waiting for a chance to enter the fray once another man had spent his load and needed some time to recuperate. Dixon Kuntz was there, waiting his turn, as was Brock Longfinger. There were a few fluffers waiting in the wings too, but they mostly looked bored. Their presence had been on the decline ever since the invention of those little blue pills.

Amber was climbing her way further up the cargo net to untie Selina, but she was moving slowly, in a post-coital haze. Either that, or she had overdone it on whatever she smoked before the shoot.

Selina was trying to be patient, but really just wanted to be let loose. She scanned the edges of the set again, fluttering inside at all the people who were watching her and her friends get off. Then she noticed something. Beyond the set, behind the crew, she saw someone in a black overcoat, wearing a black fedora. And a few feet to the left of that person stood another, slightly taller, but dressed identically. She squeezed her eyes shut for a second, then squinted to make sure she wasn't seeing things.

"Please, Amber," she said. "Untie me fast."

Selina panned her vision all the way around the set, and realized very quickly the entire island of red was surrounded. There were dozens of individuals standing in a circle, like some religious order about to begin an occult ritual.

"Come on. *Hurry,*" she said, a bit louder, panic beginning to set in. Then she buckled as something hit the cargo net hard. A moment passed before she realized nothing had hit the net—Amber had been quickly, violently pulled from it.

In a flash, it seemed, most of the crew had fallen unconscious. Some had been knocked over the head with blunt instruments, while others had been deftly injected with some sort of chemical agent from any one of a dozen hypodermic needles.

Selina looked to Gagger, who smiled at her just before someone pounced on his back, grabbing his neck and inserting a needle into it. She watched Gagger struggle for a moment, then fall unconscious to the floor. *Not again*, she thought.

The people dressed in black—the Order of Purity—quietly stepped forward into the light. Most of the actors on the red island didn't even notice.

"Foxy! Jesse!" screamed Selina, but too many men and women were screaming and moaning already, and her voice got lost in the crowd. Amber was now on the ground behind her. Selina twisted back to see her choking on a huge dildo made of ice, a man in black holding the ball-end firm against her lips. Amber convulsed beneath the man's power, suffocating. Instant tears began to stream from Selina's eyes as she watched her new friend, someone she had just orgasmed with moments ago, die before her eyes. She screamed again.

The moment seemed like an eternity, but in reality, passed quickly. It wasn't long before the actors around the perimeter saw what was happening around them, and to them. Men and women alike were being caught by surprise and either knocked out or injected with some sort of sedative. Many were being choked with ice.

Despite the fact someone was sitting on her face, Foxy noticed something in the room wasn't right, and bench-pressed the thighs of her newest friend away from her face.

"Oh shit," she screamed, as she pressed herself up with her elbows.

She yelled across the room to Jesse, who had finally lifted her face up to see what was happening. A tall, skinny guy whose name she hadn't gotten was still drilling away at her from behind. Jesse reached back in an effort to get him to stop, but he seemed to interpret that instead as "More. Faster. Deeper. Harder."

Foxy wriggled her way out from under Peckerpacker's weight, then slipped in a puddle of someone's jizz as she tried to get to her feet. She wrenched her back in the process and had to stay down for a moment.

"Selina!" she yelled.

Her friend nodded, struggling against the net. She used a foot to tap another actress on the shoulder, and she began climbing the net to untie Selina.

Jesse reached back and pressed on Skinny's hip again. He looked stoned and was sweating profusely, but he finally seemed to understand what she was after. He stopped thrusting. Then, a second later, a pointed spear of ice burst through his stomach, at the hands of the man in black who had raced up behind him. An explosion of blood splattered onto Jesse's back. It was a familiar sensation, but the wrong color. She screamed as Skinny fell away from her, then keeled over sideways, leaking fluid onto the red sheet.

Jesse somersaulted over the cushion she had propped herself up on. The attacker grabbed someone else and was stuffing an ice dildo down her throat. She looked over to the cargo net at the back of the set and saw Selina and another woman struggling to free her. Jesse ran in that direction.

Finally, the room had erupted into chaos. Dozens of people in black had invaded the red island, while several hundred porn stars tried to either run or defend themselves while completely nude and vulnerable. There were sex toys scattered about, but plastic and rubber were no match for someone with a weapon who wanted you dead.

Each of the individuals in black had at least one frozen dildo in hand. Some carried large coolers, which surely contained more. Some of the attackers had pointed spears, others had hammers and clubs. But everything was made of ice.

It wasn't easy to traverse the set quickly. With so many mattresses, couches, and cushions, the terrain varied from one step to the next. It was like trying to make your way up a downward-moving escalator. A downward-moving escalator made of marshmallows and filled with naked people and other people who were trying to kill you.

But Jesse was determined to get to her friend. Halfway there, she saw someone in black stab the woman who was helping Selina right through her chest with a sword made of ice. Her head fell back instantly, but she gripped the net tight while several spurts of blood jumped out of the exit wound. Selina hoisted herself up and gave a swift kick to the genitals of the attacker, doubling him over and knocking him to the ground beyond the set.

Nice one, Jesse thought, as she continued to make her way toward her friend. Just then, a man in black dove at her, swinging a rod of ice like a baseball bat. She ducked and lost her footing at the same time, falling down onto the big red sheet and making the man miss. His effort was enough to topple him over, and he grunted as the arm of the couch he fell onto slammed into his side.

"Filthy whore!" he yelled through the stocking that covered his face. Then another starlet kicked him in the face, shutting him up for the time being.

Eventually, Jesse made it through the obstacle course and got to the cargo net.

"I thought you'd never get here," Selina said. Jesse climbed up the net quickly and managed to get Selina untied in a matter of seconds.

"These other chicks can't figure out knots?" said Jesse. "Where's the bag?"

"What do you mean? I gave it to Foxy. Remember?"

"Shit, that's right," said Jesse. She looked across the island and spotted Foxy. She was taking on several attackers with kicks. "Foxy! You got the bag?"

Foxy delivered a side-kick to the balls of a man in black, dropping him instantly.

"What are you talking about? I gave it to you!"

"Oh fuck," said Jesse under her breath, suddenly remembering the moment in question, and the fact she had tucked the bag behind the cushions where she had been lying until very recently. Her last orgasm must have scrambled her brain a bit. "You ready to move, Selina? We need to head back the way I came."

Selina turned to her left, grabbed a handful of red sheet, and ripped a hole. She reached through and yanked free a pair of couch cushions from within, then tore two slits in the fabric of each of them. She slid her arm in one hole and out the other, then raised it to demonstrate her idea.

"Use it like a shield," she said, handing the second cushion to Jesse. "Better than nothing, right?"

Jesse nodded.

The pair took off, bouncing their way down the soft red mountain. An attacker came at them from Selina's side, but she used her cushion to deflect the path of the ice dildo headed for her face, then kicked the assailant's knee backward with a satisfying crunch.

"Métetelo por el culo!" she screamed.

Another person in black approached from Jesse's side. Running alongside her, he touched her shoulder, then grabbed a handful of candy-red hair in an effort to stop her movement. Jesse shifted course, spinning him around, then off balance. When he hit the red sheet, she stomped on his stomach with a bare heel, knocking the wind out of him.

Selina and Jesse continued to bound their way through the tangle of naked porn stars and black-clad killers. They avoided physical contact as much as possible, but still had to deliver a few punches and kicks along the way. It took longer than expected, but eventually they made it back to where Jesse had been stationed during the shoot, before everything had devolved from a free-for-all fuck-fest to an orgy of assault and murder.

"What the fuck? Where is it?" Jesse said, panicked. She tossed pillows and cushions left and right. "It was right here!"

"You sure we're in the right spot?" asked Selina.

"Yeah, yeah, I'm sure. I was bent over that pile of cushions, and I could see the handle of the bag poking out from right here. *Where the fuck did it go?!"*

"Jesse," said Selina.

"What?"

"Jesse!" Selina said again, this time more urgent.

"What?!" Jesse spat, annoyed.

"Looking for this?" asked a male voice. Jesse looked up. A man in a black overcoat, with a black stocking over his face and a black fedora on his head, stood about twenty feet further up the red set, perched with his legs wide across the arm and the back of a red couch. He had one hand up high. A duffel bag dangled from his fingers.

In the other hand, the man held a massive tube of ice, four feet long, thick, and shaped like a penis. It had a slight curve to it, which Jesse and Selina both noticed as he raised the tip slowly from his feet up past his waist.

"Hand it over, asshole," Jesse said.

"Come and get it," the man said. A drop of water fell from the tip of his weapon.

"What now?" Selina whispered. Jesse didn't respond. They both scanned the red surface around them, searching for something other than a pillow to use as a weapon. There was nothing within reach. "You want to charge him? If we both hit him at the same time, he can't hurt us both."

"Can't think of any better options right now," said Jesse. "Ready?"

Selina nodded. Both women tossed their long hair over their

shoulders and raised their respective shield-cushions to block as much of their bodies as possible.

Just then, a *whoosh-whoosh-whoosh* sound sliced through the screams and grunts in the room, and before Selina and Jesse could move, a big purple rubber dildo collided with the back of the man's head. He was knocked instantly unconscious, and fell from the couch, then tumbled down toward Selina and Jesse.

Across the room, far beyond where he had stood, was Foxy, with a second rubber dildo in her hand, ready to throw just like the first one. It wasn't necessary.

"Foxy!" Jesse and Selina cheered in unison. They high-fived each other and smiled wide, but there was no time to celebrate. Across the room, Foxy was immediately approached by another attacker, a figure in black wielding a sharpened shaft of ice like a katana. She raised the dildo in her hand the same way.

"Shit," said Selina. "We're surrounded." Jesse looked around and saw what Selina did. A ring of murderers in black were closing in on them in all directions. She bounded over to the fallen assailant and snatched the bag from his now-weak fingers. The man grunted, and she delivered a heel kick to his ribs.

Jesse unzipped the bag and reached inside. Wood and metal knocked and clanged against each other as Jesse extracted her hand from the bag. It held one of three sharp axes.

"Ready to do this?" she asked, handing the weapon to Selina.

"Let's go," said Selina with a smile. *"Chop-chop!"*

"Hey! Foxy!" Jesse shouted. Foxy was sword-fighting someone dressed in black with a green rubber dildo and looked like she could use some help. "We're coming!"

"Anytime you're ready!" Foxy exclaimed. She kept focused on her fight.

"In the meantime, catch!" yelled Jesse. Then she spun like an Olympian and heaved one of the axes in Foxy's direction. The tool spun end-over-end in the air, not unlike the purple dildo Foxy had taken someone out with just a few moments prior.

Foxy ducked a swing by her attacker and rolled left onto a pile of heart-shaped pillows. Then, from down on one knee, Foxy jumped straight up in the air as high as she could and came down with the axe in her hand.

"Now we're talking," she said.

The man took another swing at her, but she met this one with the head of the axe, and the tube of ice snapped into two pieces. Momentarily stunned, the man froze. Foxy chuckled, then spun to deliver a roundhouse kick to the man's side. Then, planting her feet, she swung at him again, this time burying the head of the axe into his head, crumpling the shape of his fedora, and splitting his skull down the middle. Blood and a few small chunks of brain matter sprayed back onto her face and chest, but Foxy didn't even blink. That was the most satisfying thing she had done in a while.

"I'm coming to you!" she yelled to her friends.

"Meet in the middle!" Selina responded.

A few moments later, the three women had all made their way to the center of the red island. They quickly positioned themselves back-to-back, axes out, and prepared for the circle of attackers closing in on them.

"Freeze them!" screamed one of the figures in black.

The Order of Purity continued cinching their circle smaller and smaller. Each member of the cult was dressed the same way, and they each held in their hands at least one implement made of ice. There were ice dildos ranging anywhere from one foot long to four. Many of the shafts were shaped like dicks, some perfectly straight, others with slight upward curves. Some even had sculpted veins running their entire lengths. Some were sharpened to lethal points, while others retained more realistic, blunt Vader-helmet tips. They all had frozen testicles at their bases.

But others had that not-exactly-realistic sex-toy look, with bulbous ends, and a variety of bumps and ridges. One person even held a long cord with a series of evenly spaced frozen spheres attached to it. He swung one end of it in a circle, like some sort of ninja weapon.

They had come to purify as many souls as possible, but for the moment, their attention was focused on the three women with axes.

"Purify!" yelled one of the men. "Purify!" screamed another. *"Kill the filthy fornicator-slut-whores!"* exclaimed a third. And they attacked.

Fifteen feet away, Jesse spotted her friend Riley, doing her best to fend off an assailant with a sharpened spike of ice in his hand.

"I'm on my way, Riley!" Jesse yelled.

But a second attacker snuck up behind Riley, and he was so

fast, Jesse didn't even have time to warn her. The man in black knocked Riley across the back of the head with a blunt tube of frozen water. The first man then dove at her with his weapon and quickly buried the icicle in her throat. Riley's scream dissipated into a weak gurgle as several heaves of blood spurted from her neck, forming a small puddle of red on her clavicle and beneath her head.

"*Noooooo!*" screamed Jesse, too far away to do anything. Riley convulsed on a small pile of cushions and quickly faded away. "*Riley!*" Jesse screamed, even though she knew it was already too late.

In an instant, clarity took over, and Jesse channeled her sadness and anger through her hands. She stepped forward toward the ring of attackers and began swinging as they closed in.

The moments that followed were all red. It was as if the women had been possessed by the spirit of Gagger's lumberjack father to become experts with the bladed weapons in their hands.

When someone lunged at Jesse, she leapt up and met him with a kick to the midsection, before bringing her axe down on the back of his head.

"Fuck you!" she said.

When a man with an eighteen-inch cock made of ice came at Selina, she knocked his weapon away with the blunt side of her axe blade, then swung back and buried the sharp edge into the crook of his shoulder.

"Chingate!" she said.

When a man charged at Foxy, his ice-sword raised up high,

she quickly flipped her axe upside-down, ducked, and swung upward from down low, burying the blade in the man's crotch.

"Nice axe wound, asshole," she said.

The bloodshed continued for several minutes, as naked, blood-spattered porn stars ran, frantic, in every direction. Jesse, Foxy, and Selina continued their three-pronged attack, and managed it well. The Order of Purity's frozen weapons were no match for a trio of lumberjacks' axes.

Soon, the three women were slicked with red from their hairlines to their ankles, blending in with the red of the set. Various bodies, all dressed in black, lay motionless in a circle around them, some mortally wounded, others hacked to pieces. Finally, it seemed, the nightmare was over.

The hundred or so surviving porn stars surrounded the set and slowly climbed back up to offer hugs to the trio of axe-wielding saviors.

Some began unmasking the bodies of the cult members. Many of them were unfamiliar, though a few were recognized as crew members who had obviously infiltrated the industry as part of a long game that had come to a head that afternoon.

Jesse made her way over to Riley's now-lifeless body and grasped her hand.

"I'm so sorry," she whispered, tears beginning to well in her eyes. The spike of ice that had ended Riley's life had already melted enough to fall from the wound in her neck.

Through the bloodshed of the last several minutes, Jesse had kept an eye on the man who delivered the fatal blow to her friend, and she had made sure she was the one to bury her axe in his chest. She stepped over to where he lay now and crouched down beside his body.

She grabbed the bottom of the stocking covering his face and pulled upward to reveal the face of Officer Richard Knowles.

"Fucking Dick," she said, then stood back up, and began swinging her axe down onto his head. In only a few seconds, Jesse delivered a dozen blows to the officer's face, turning it into a wet mound of red mash.

Foxy and Selina made their way over to her and managed to stop her from swinging again. Foxy wrapped an arm around Jesse's body as Selina extracted the weapon from her hands.

"Stop," said Foxy. "It's all over." Jesse began crying, then turned around to her friends, and the three of them embraced, sticky with the coagulating blood of dozens of now-dead assailants.

2 0

Two Weeks Later

"I'm glad you're feeling better, hon," Jesse said into the phone. Gagger was on the other end. "Bad as that day was, things could've been a lot worse."

"Thanks to you and the girls," he said. "I just wish I could've helped. I've taken a lot of stuff in my throat over the years, but that needle was something else. I still have a bruise on my neck, for fuck's sake."

They talked for a few more minutes, then the doorbell rang.

"Okay, I gotta run," Jesse said. "The girls are here. Lunch tomorrow?"

"Sounds good."

Jesse hung up and answered the door to her apartment. Selina and Foxy stood on the stoop and smiled.

"Hey, girl," said Foxy.

"I made churros," said Selina, raising a rubber container for display.

"Oooh," said Jesse. "Gimme." She stepped aside to let her friends enter.

"Looks like you got some mail," said Foxy, handing over a small stack of envelopes.

"Thanks. There's coffee if you want it."

"So, any shoots lined up?" asked Foxy, sipping from a mug. "Mmm, this is good shit." She closed her eyes for a moment, savoring the taste.

"No, nothing yet," replied Jesse. "Everybody's still kind of shell-shocked. I hope something comes together soon, though." She held up her mail pile. "I've got bills to pay."

"Tell me about it," said Selina, reaching for the container of churros on the table, having grown tired of waiting for someone else to open it.

"Oh, sorry," said Jesse, jumping up. "I'll get some napkins." She dropped the mail on the table beside the churros. "We're eating all of these now, right?"

Selina responded with a smile. She had already finished her first.

"Well, at least one of these isn't a bill," said Foxy, sliding the mail off to the side.

"Oh yeah?" called Jesse from the kitchen.

"Looks like a letter to me."

Jesse returned with a handful of paper napkins. She handed one to each of her friends and dropped the rest of the stack on the table.

"A letter? Who sends letters anymore?" Jesse grabbed a churro and stuck it between her teeth, then picked up the envelope in question. She slid a finger under the flap and tore it open, removing a tri-folded greeting card from inside.

She flipped open the first panel to reveal a handwritten note. In part, it read:

'While we never agreed with all of our daughter's choices, we respected her wishes, and we were thankful she had someone like you in her life to help steer her away from real trouble. We always hoped she would come home and decide to go back to school, so we kept her college fund intact. Now that she's left us all, however, we wanted to put the money toward something in her memory. Though you may not have realized it, she loved and respected you so much. Please accept the enclosed check with our most sincere thanks. Do some good with it.'

"Oh . . . wow . . ." Jesse said with a mouthful of churro. She chewed and swallowed and placed the rest of it on a napkin on the table. "It's from Riley's parents."

"Oh yeah?" said Foxy.

Jesse opened the second flap of the card and removed the check tucked inside. Her eyes grew wide, and her lips parted. She dropped herself into a soft chair, needing to sit down.

"You okay?" Foxy asked.

She and Selina walked over to where Jesse was now seated. Jesse handed over the card, and they read through it together.

When they were finished, Jesse held up the check for them to see.

"Mierda," said Selina. "That's a lot of money."

"Yeah," said Jesse, stunned.

"So . . . time for you to start Jinx Pix?" Selina said.

"I guess so," Jesse said, her eyes still wide. *"But I'm not going to do it."*

"Wait, what?" said Foxy, in disbelief. "This is what you've been dreaming of. It's something we *need.*"

"Exactly," Jesse explained. "I'm not going to do it. *We are.*" Selina and Foxy turned to look at each other, as smiles crept onto their faces.

"We're in this together," Jesse continued. "Three-way equal partnership. Okay?"

Jesse's friends nodded.

"But we'll have to change the name," Jesse said. "I never really liked Jinx Pix anyway."

"Hmmm," said Foxy, thinking for a moment. "How about . . . *Triple Axe Productions?* 'T-A-P. TAP that ass.'"

"I like it," said Selina. "'*You can watch us fuck. But you can't fuck with us.*'"

"Yes," said Jesse. She stood up and hugged her friends. "Let's do it."

21

Across town, two men stood outside an abandoned warehouse. It had been a gray day and the sun was now setting behind a wall of dark clouds. They heard the soft crunch of gravel in the distance. Eventually a black car with tinted windows appeared and rolled to a stop a few feet in front of them. A figure dressed in black emerged from the back seat.

"A sad day indeed," he said, acknowledging the events surrounding what the adult industry had dubbed *The Big Bang*. "So many of our Brothers and Sisters now gone."

The other men nodded.

"But at least they know now they died as martyrs for a noble cause. A cause we must continue to fight for, at all costs."

The man speaking paused for a moment.

"I understand you've brought some new recruits into the fold. I'd like to meet them."

The two other men escorted their leader, the head of the Order of Purity, into the warehouse, where they had assembled a group of men and women. They had been flown in from all over the country, and they were all eager to join the fight.

The leader was surprised his charges had done so well. The warehouse was nearly filled, with hundreds of people standing shoulder-to-shoulder. He approached a makeshift podium.

"Hello, Brothers and Sisters," he said.

Acknowledgements

Thanks to Gina Renzi, Adam Cesare, C.V. Hunt, Andersen
Prunty, Matt Serafini, Patrick Lacey, and Jason Neugent, who
all helped in one way or another to make this book come. Come
out, I mean.

Scott Cole is a writer, artist, and graphic designer living in Philadelphia. He likes old radio dramas, old horror comics, weird movies, cold weather, coffee, and a few other things too. Find him on Facebook and Twitter. If you dare.

Other Grindhouse Press Titles

Made in the USA
Las Vegas, NV
02 June 2022